LADY GUNSMITH

2

The Three Graves of Roxy Doyle

LADY GUNSMITH

2

The Three Graves of Roxy Doyle

J. R. Roberts

SPEAKING VOLUMES, LLC
NAPLES, FLORIDA
2017

The Three Graves of Roxy Doyle

ISBN 978-1-62815-709-3

PART ONE

Chapter One

Roxy Doyle rode into Sunset, New Mexico at midday. She had been riding aimlessly for some time now—was it days? Weeks? She couldn't be sure. All she knew was that the trail in her longtime search for her missing father, famed bounty hunter Gavin Doyle, had gone cold. She had no clue as to where to go, or who to talk to, next. So she just rode . . .

When she saw the sign announcing the town of Sunset up ahead, she decided she was tired of sleeping on the ground and could use a hot meal and a bed.

As she entered the town limits she rode past Sunset's version of Boot Hill, and noticed there was a burial going on. People were crowded around the site. The odd thing was that there were so many of them, and they didn't seem particularly upset. In fact, as she rode closer she thought the atmosphere seemed decidedly more like a party than a funeral. It was enough to rouse her curiosity, so she reined in, tied her horse to a sapling, and started up the hill.

People were loud, some arguing, some simply yelling, many of them punching the air, slapping each other on the back.

She heard someone say, "This is gonna put us on the map!"

Another man said, "Sunset's gonna be famous!"

Apparently, somebody important had died, and rather than being sad, the town thought it was going to do them some good. A decidedly bad attitude to have about somebody's death, she thought.

Now she was more determined than ever to see who was being buried. As she pushed her way to the front, the crowd actually started to disperse.

"Come on," someone yelled, "drinks at the saloon are on the house for the next hour!"

Men and women yelled their approval, and the crowd started to move down the hill. Roxy now found herself moving against the tide, as she continued to work her way toward the grave.

Finally, her pushing and the crowd's thinning out brought her into the clear. She could see the fresh grave, marked with a crude headstone—a wooden board with writing on it. She had to move around to the foot of the grave in order to read the letters. When she did, she froze.

HERE LIES ROXY DOYLE
LADY GUNSMITH
SHOT TO DEATH IN
SUNSET, NEW MEXICO

The grave was hers, only she wasn't in. She was standing at the foot of it, reading her own epitaph.

She looked around, but most of the crowd had now worked its way down to the street, and was apparently heading for the saloon. The only person still on the hill with her was a man in a dark suit, and a white collar, holding a Bible.

"Father?" she said.

He smiled. "I'm not a priest, just a minister. My name is Peter Winston."

"Mr. Winston," she said. "Is that really Lady Gunsmith in the grave?"

"It is," he said. "She came to town several days ago, made her presence known immediately."

"How did she do that?"

"Well," he said, "that mass of red hair, the green eyes, the way she, uh, looked," he moved his hands up and down his body, "and then there was the way she wore her gun . . . it was no secret."

At the moment Roxy had her own mass of red hair piled on top of her head and stuffed beneath her hat.

"The way she wore her gun?"

"You know, like a gunfighter?"

"You know how a gunfighter wears their gun?" she asked.

"Ah, no," he admitted, "but somebody said so."

"Did she do anything else?" she asked. "Say anything else?"

"Well," the minister said, "she killed a man. Right out there in the street. Outdrew him. He never got his gun out."

"Was it a fair fight?" she asked.

"Apparently. I mean, they both had guns, but the man she killed? He was no gunfighter, just a big mouth in a bar. She coulda walked away, but she called him out into the street, shot him dead."

"You got a sheriff in this town?"

"Sure," the minister said. "He was there, but he didn't do anything. Not against her."

4

"I see," Roxy said. "So then, how did she end up in a grave?"

"The way most of these people end up in a grave," he said. "The way Wild Bill Hickok ended up in his."

"You mean . . .?"

"Yes, Ma'am," Winston said. "Somebody shot her in the back."

Chapter Two

The minister left Roxy on Boot Hill alone, and she stayed there for a few more moments. After all, how many times does somebody get the chance to read their own headstone? But when she'd finally had enough, she walked down the hill to her horse, and mounted up.

She rode down the street, passed a saloon that was obviously full of revelers, people who were just thrilled that Roxy Doyle, the Lady Gunsmith, had been killed in their town.

She kept riding until she spotted the sheriff's office, and decided it should be her next stop after Boot Hill.

After tying off her horse in front, she mounted the boardwalk and entered the office. There were two men inside, both of whom turned to face her as she entered. One had a deputy's badge on, and one a sheriff's badge. The deputy was handsome, in his twenties, the sheriff older, probably late thirties, rugged looking. He was holding a handful of posters in his hands, and they were obviously going through them.

"Sorry to interrupt," she said.

Both men stared at her for a few moments, and then the sheriff said, "No problem, Ma'am. What can we do for you, today?"

"I just rode into town," she said, "right past Boot Hill. Seems like there was a party going on there. That's not something you usually see at a cemetery."

"Oh, yeah," the sheriff said, shaking his head. "That's not our town at its best hour, not by a long sight. Please, don't judge us by that."

"What are you talkin' about, Sheriff?" the deputy asked, breaking in. "I mean, the shopkeepers and ranchers around here, they're pretty excited. This is gonna bring a lot of people to town, you know—"

"Johnny," the sheriff said, "shut up and go make your rounds, will ya?"

"Huh? Oh, yeah, sure." The deputy turned to look at Roxy. "Ma'am."

"Deputy."

She waited until the younger man had left the office before addressing the sheriff, again.

"I heard what happened," she said. "That . . . Roxy Doyle killed a man in the street in a fair fight?"

"Is that what you heard?"

"Only maybe it wasn't a fair fight?"

"You heard that too, huh?" He walked around his desk and sat down. "And I guess you heard that I didn't do anythin' about it."

"Somethin' like that," she said, "but I was wondering who shot . . . who shot Roxy in the back?"

The sheriff frowned at her use of the first name.

"Did you know 'er?" he asked.

"You could say that."

Now the sheriff really studied her.

"You look a little like 'er," he said, finally. "Are you . . . her sister, maybe?"

"No," Roxy said, "closer than that."

"Closer?" he asked. "What's closer than a sister? You're way too young to be her mother."

"Not her mother," Roxy said, shaking her head. "Closer than that, too."

"Well, now you've got me," the sheriff said. "If you're not her sister, and not her mother, but you're closer than that, then . . ." He let it trail off as he frowned at her.

She smiled. "Now you're getting it. Let me help you a little further." She took off her hat, loosened her hair and shook it out, letting it fall to her shoulders. Then she put her hat on his desk, so he could see the turquoise hatband.

"Come on," he said, "you're . . ."

"I'm Roxy Doyle," she said.

He sat back in his chair.

"You're Lady Gunsmith?"

"That's right."

"Then who's that in the grave?"

"I don't know," she said. "Obviously, somebody pretending to be me."

"Now wait, wait," he said, putting his hands out and moving forward in his chair, "suppose you rode into town, saw that she'd been buried, and you're the one pretending to be her, not the other way around."

"Really?" she asked. "With my red hair and green eyes, I just happen to ride into town today? Isn't that a bit of a coincidence?"

"However you wanna play it, it's a coincidence," he pointed out.

"You're right there," she admitted, "but the way you're putting it, it'd be a helluva coincidence."

"Okay," he said, sitting back again, "can you prove who you are?"

"How am I supposed to do that?" she asked him. "Do you want me to do some trick shooting for you? Or how about I kill somebody?"

"Do you have a letter that might have been written to you?" he asked. "Somethin' in your pocket or your saddlebags with your name on it?"

"Nobody writes me letters," she said. "I don't have anything like that. I travel too much."

"Okay, something else, then," he said. "Somebody who knows you, who can vouch for you?"

"I've never been to your town before," she said. "I don't know anybody."

"Then as far as I know," he said, "you're just a young woman who looks like Lady Gunsmith, who is now lying in a grave on Boot Hill."

"Unless I can prove different."

"Exactly."

"So what's your name?" she asked.

"I'm Jack Taggert."

"How do I know that?"

"Well," he said, "for one thing, people here will vouch for me. And then—"

"Okay," she said, "forget that. Let's just put that question aside for the moment and talk about something else."

"Like what?" he asked. "Is there somethin' else on your mind?"

"Yes," she said, "I'd like to know who shot your Roxy Doyle?"

Chapter Three

"I don't know who shot her."

"How'd it happen?" Roxy asked.

"Look," the sheriff said, "sit down. You want some coffee?"

"Sure," Roxy said, "I'll take some coffee."

The sheriff went to a stove in a corner, poured two mugs of coffee, brought them back to the desk and handed Roxy one.

"Sorry, I don't have any milk or sugar," he said, sitting behind his desk, again. "I drink it just the way it is."

"Black's fine," she said. "Thank you." She sat back and drank.

"The shootin' happened at night," the lawman said, taking up his story. "She was walkin' in the street, probably headin' back to her hotel. There was a shot, and that was it, By the time I got there she was face down in the street, dead"

"One shot?' Roxy asked. "In the dark?"

"That's right."

"It sounds like somebody knew what they were doing." She drank more coffee.

"Exactly. We took her to the undertaker's, and that was it. We didn't know who to contact, so we decided just to bury her here in town."

"And then spread the word."

"That's not me," he said, "that started with the editor of our newspaper. It was his idea. He said he'd publish a story in our paper, the Sunset Gazette, and then word would get out and people would come."

"And the people of this town liked that idea?"

"They loved it," he said. "The mayor went for it whole hog. They all think Sunset's gonna be famous."

"And what do you think?"

"I think it's a helluva thing to be famous for."

She finished her coffee and put the empty mug on the edge of his desk.

"More?"

"That was fine, thanks," she said. "What are you doing to find out who killed her?"

"I asked some questions," he said. "I checked the buildings across from where she was shot. But then I was shut down."

"What do you mean?"

"The mayor told me to forget it. He said it doesn't matter who killed her, all that matters is that she was killed here."

"That doesn't sound right."

"Not to me, either," he admitted.

"Well," she said, standing up, "if I can't convince you who I am, there's not much you can do for me."

"What do you want me to do for you?"

"I'd like to know who shot me," she said. "Or who tried to shoot me. I'd like to know who this woman was who was impersonating me, and how long she was doing it. And if she's done anything I'm going to get blamed for."

"So what are you gonna do?"

"Stay in town a while," she said. "Ask some questions."

He frowned.

"What's wrong?"

"Well," he said, "if you were only pretending to be Lady Gunsmith, I can't see that you'd stay in town asking questions, just to make it seem like you really were her."

"So what? You believe me now?"

"Not quite," he said. "Let's just say I've got an open mind."

"Did you talk to her much while she was here?" Roxy asked. "And how long was she here, by the way?"

"She was here for several days," he said. "I had one meetin' with her, tellin' her I didn't want her killin' anybody in my town."

"I guess she didn't listen."

"But I didn't want her to get killed here, either," he pointed out.

"I guess you're the only one," she said.

"Look," he said, "tuck your hair back under your hat, and don't register in a hotel as Roxy Doyle."

"Why's that?"

"If somebody in town thinks they killed Lady Gunsmith, and then you start claimin' that you're Lady Gunsmith" he said, "they may just try to kill you, just to make sure they got the right one."

"On the other hand," she said, "if I register under my own name and somebody tries to kill me, I may just get lucky and catch a killer."

"Or unlucky, and catch a bullet."

"Well," she said, "I'll think about what you've said between here and the hotel. When I get there, I'll decide what to do."

"What about the hair?"

She gathered up her hair and tucked it back beneath her hat.

"For now," she said.

"That's fine," he said. "I don't want another beautiful woman gettin' killed in my town."

"Was she beautiful?" Roxy asked.

"Well," he said, "I thought so—until I saw you."

Chapter Four

After she walked her horse to the hotel and approached the desk, she decided not to register under her own name. For now, she'd keep quiet about who she was. For a moment she considered registering as "Belle Starr" but that might start some trouble, as well. In the end she registered as "Mary Smith."

She accepted her key from the smiling clerk, put her saddlebags and rifle in her room, and then walked her mount to the nearest livery.

"Wow," the hostler said, "you remind me of somebody."

"Somebody who got killed here in town?" she asked.

"That's right," the older man said. "Lady Gunsmith. How did you know?"

"I rode in past the cemetery," she said. "Saw the crowd. Did she have her horse here?"

"Yep, she did. I still got it, in fact."

"Do you have her saddle, and saddlebags?"

"Got the saddle," the man said. "Don't know who got her saddlebags. Folks was scramblin' for souvenirs, though. Could be anybody."

Roxy left the livery, thinking about those saddlebags. If she could find them, maybe there'd be something inside to tell her who the woman really was.

She passed a saloon on the way back to the hotel, decided to stop in and wash away some of the trail dust from her throat with a cold beer.

As she entered she attracted the attention of the male customers, as well as the girls working the floor. At the bar the bartender gave her a big, gap-toothed grin.

"Jesus," he said, "if she wasn't already dead and buried I woulda thought you was the Lady Gunsmith."

"Can I have a beer?" she asked.

"Sure thing, honey." He drew the beer and set it in front of her.

Normally, she would have told him not to call her honey, but instead she simply asked, "Is she dead?"

"As can be," the man said. "Somebody plugged her right in the back, the same day she gunned Homer Mason."

"What was Homer's problem?" she asked.

"Homer had a big mouth and a slow hand," the bartender said.

"Too bad for him."

"Yup."

"So you must've seen her while she was here," Roxy said. "She come in here for a drink?"

"Nope, she did her drinkin' at the Live Oak Saloon, couple a blocks away. Guess she went in there first and liked it, never got this far."

"Too bad for you," she said.

"You got that right," he said. "My place coulda been the one she had her last drink in before she died."

16

"That right?" Roxy asked. "She was in the Live Oak just before she got shot?"

"That's what George Buckwold says," the man answered. "He owns the Live Oak."

"Maybe I should go and have a look."

"We got better beer, though."

She drank down half of it and put the mug on the bar.

"I guess if it was cold, it'd be pretty good." She tossed a coin on the bar. "Thanks."

She left the little no name saloon and walked the couple of blocks to the Live Oak. As she entered she saw a hand-written sign by the door. It said:

THIS IS THE PLACE WHERE
LADY GUNSMITH HAD HER LAST DRINK
BEFORE SOMEBODY PLUGGED HER.

She was tempted to whip off her hat, let her hair down and cause a ruckus, but she controlled the urge. Instead, she just walked to the bar.

The Live Oak was bigger and busier than the other saloon. Lots of men bellied up to the bar, others seated at tables, were drinking or playing poker. More girls worked the floor, younger and prettier ones.

Most of the men turned to look at her, then took a second look because of her resemblance to the dead Lady Gunsmith.

The men at the bar gave her some space, smiled at her as she stepped between two of them.

"Beer," she said to the bartender.

"Comin' up, Missy."

That wasn't much better than "honey" but she let it pass, too—for the moment.

"Let me buy the lady's drink, Ted," the man on her right said.

She looked at him. In his 40's, he was dressed like a cowhand, which was probably what he was, judging from the dust on his clothes, and the smell.

"Well," she said, "thank you, kindly."

"My pleasure, Ma'am."

She sipped the beer, and this time it was cold.

"What brings you to town?" the man asked.

Roxy hoped he didn't notice that she'd moved a little further from him, trying to get away from the smell.

"I heard there was some excitement here," she said. "You know anything about that?'

"Oh, you mean Lady Gunsmith gettin' herself killed," he said. "Oh yeah, that's gonna make this town famous."

"You really think so?" she asked.

"That's what everybody's sayin'," he said. "You know, you look a little like her."

"Really?"

"Yeah," he said, "but you're a lot prettier."

"Did you see her?" Roxy asked. "Up close, I mean."

"Well, no, not really," he said. "Not right up close, but I seen her around town, struttin' her stuff until somebody put 'er in the ground."

"So you don't know any more than that?"

"'fraid not, little lady," he said, "but why don't we go somewhere else and I'll show you what I do know."

"Huh," she said, "that offer doesn't interest me, at all."

"It—what?"

"And could you move a little further away from me?" she asked. "The smell is starting to make my brain feel numb."

He stared at her, his mouth open, for a few seconds, until she turned away from him and faced the bar, concentrating on her cold beer.

Chapter Five

"That was a little rough," the bartender said. "I think you hurt Willie's feelins'."

She looked at him to see if he was serious, and decided he wasn't.

"Willie needs a bath," she said, "real bad."

"Willie always needs a bath," he said. "But he don't take kindly to bein' embarrassed."

Roxy looked to see Willie had joined a few friends at one of the tables. They were talking, and he was pointing her way.

This was just what she didn't need, some cowpokes starting trouble.

"Who're those fellas?" she asked.

"Them's Willie's friends," the bartender said. "They ride for the Bar S, out South of town."

"Are they liable to do something stupid?" she asked.

"Every chance they get," he said. "You'd probably be better off leavin'."

"I think you're right." She paid for her beer. "Thanks."

"Sure."

She went through the batwings, hoping Willie and his friends weren't going to follow her. Maybe they hadn't consumed enough alcohol to do something really stupid . . . yet.

***

Roxy spent the afternoon walking around town, trying to eavesdrop on conversations, since the shooting of lady Gunsmith was the hot topic of the day. Folks really did seem to believe that her death was going to put their town on the map. In fact, she must have heard that phrase half-a-dozen times.

Later in the day she stopped at a small café on a side street, hoping to avoid drawing any attention to herself. Unfortunately, even with her hair tucked up beneath her hat, she was just too beautiful not to be seen—especially by men.

As she was shown to a table she was the center of attention for the few people who were also dining there.

She ordered a bowl of beef stew and ate it without removing her hat.

When she was done she paid her bill and got out of there fast. She walked to go back to her hotel to regroup, and decide what to do. It's a rough day when everybody in town is talking about your death.

At the hotel she entered the lobby and headed for the stairs, but the clerk waved at her.

"What is it?" she asked.

"Somebody left a message for you, Ma'am."

She took her foot off the first step and walked over to the desk.

"What is it?"

"I dunno," he said. "It's in here." He grabbed an envelope from behind the desk and handed it to her.

"Thanks."

21

She went up the stairs, waited until she was in her room to open it.

It said:

IF YOU WANT MORE INFORMATION ABOUT LADY GUNSMITH, MEET ME AT THE WILLOW STREET LIVERY STABLE AT MIDNIGHT. COME ALONE.

It wasn't signed.

Come alone? Who would she come with? She didn't know anybody in town.

Was this from Willie? Were he and his friends trying to draw her out so they could get back at her for embarrassing him? Or did somebody really have information for her? She decided she had to chance it to find out.

She had many hours to kill before midnight, so she took a nap. She knew she'd wake up in plenty of time to make what was now an appointment. Her inner clock would not let her miss it.

Chapter Six

She left the hotel at eleven-thirty, giving herself plenty of time to find Willow Street, and the livery stable. Also, she was hoping she might even get there first.

Locating the livery with no trouble she circled it first, trying to see if anyone was there, waiting for her. Finally, she decided it was time to go in, just as the moon was high and bright.

She walked to the front door, grabbed and pulled, found it unlocked. Inside, there was a lamp burning, which could have meant somebody was already there, or the lamp had been burning for a long time.

She walked in, ready for anything, like three drunken cowpokes coming at her. Luckily, that wasn't what happened.

A man stepped from the shadows into the light of the lamp. He was tall, and older, perhaps as old as 70. He wore a black coat and a black hat, both of which had seen better days.

"I'm glad you came," he said.

"You've got some information for me?"

"That depends," he said. "Can you pay for it?"

"Why would I do that?"

"Because," he said, "I happen to know that you're Lady Gunsmith."

"And how do you know that?"

"I've seen you before."

"Where? When?"

"A few years back, in a town called Colton, Montana."

Roxy thought back. She remembered going to Colton because somebody told her they had seen her father there. It turned out not to be true, but she'd also been forced to kill a man while she was in town.

"I saw you in action," he said, "and I was impressed."

"What's your name?"

"I'm Xander Tyler."

"I don't know that name."

"You wouldn't," he said. "I'm nobody, just a man tryin' to last."

"And that's why you want to sell me some information?"

"The man nodded.

"Do you know the woman who was impersonating me?"

"No, I didn't."

"Do you know who shot her?"

"I don't, no."

"Then what do you have to sell me?"

"You'll have to pay me to find out."

"And if I don't like what I paid for?"

"You're not gonna like what you pay for," he told her, "but I know you won't try to take the money back. I saw the kind of person you are in Colton. You ain't changed since then, have you?"

"I'm afraid I've changed quite a bit since then," she told him.

"Well, then," he said, "I guess we'll both be takin' a chance."

"I don't have much money," she said.

"I'll take whatever you can give me."

"Five dollars?"

"If that's all you can spare, I'll take it," he said.

She reached into her pocket, came out with all the money she had at that moment; ten dollars. She held out five of it, and he walked forward with long strides and took it. Standing right there in front of her she realized he was over six-and-a-half feet tall. If she'd seen him in Colton, she would remember.

"Okay," she said "what have you got for me?"

"There's a town ten miles from here," he said, "called Telegraph. You're gonna wanna ride there tomorrow."

"And why would I want to do that?"

"Because," he said, "yesterday they buried Lady Gunsmith on their Boot Hill."

Chapter Seven

The next morning Roxy checked out of the hotel, saddled her horse and headed ten miles South, to the town of Telegraph . . .

Telegraph, New Mexico was a slightly smaller town than Sunset, but may have looked more prosperous. She didn't know what it was, it just felt that way. The street was cleaner, and there wasn't a dirty window in sight.

It was early, and the town seemed sleepy. There was no partying going on in the street.

As soon as she arrived she looked for and found Boot Hill, just outside of town. She tied off her horse, ascended the hill and started looking at gravesites. She finally found one that was fresh, with a hand-written wooden marker on it that read:

SHOT TO DEATH IN TELEGRAPH
LADY GUNSMITH

Short and to the point. Now she needed to hear this story from somebody.

She walked back down the hill, remounted her horse and rode into town.

As she had done in Sunset, she sought out the sheriff's office, found it, and dismounted. Only this time she encountered a locked door.

Looking around, not seeing any people, she wondered where everyone was. If they were so excited to be "the" town that Lady Gunsmith was killed in, why wasn't there some sort of celebration.

Finally, she decided to try the nearest saloon and see what that got her—and what it got her was another locked door.

Now she figured the whole town was probably off in the same place, and since it wasn't the cemetery, it could only be one place.

She mounted up and rode . . .

***

She found the church on the far side of town, dismounted and went up the steps. She could hear voices inside and reached for the door, then stopped. If the whole town was inside, she couldn't go in there. She'd have all eyes on her, and she didn't want that, unsure how a stranger would be received. Especially one who resembled their Lady Gunsmith.

She went back down the steps to her horse, and stopped. There had to be somewhere else to go, where'd she find somebody . . . anybody.

Then it occurred to her.

Who wouldn't go to church?

***

She found the whorehouse by looking for one of the largest houses in town. Whorehouses usually had two floors, so the girls could take the men upstairs to their rooms.

She dismounted in front, tied the horse off again, and knocked on the front door. A girl in a filmy robe answered and looked her up and down.

"Honey," she said, "if you're wantin' a job I can tell you that Madam Rosie will take you in a minute."

"Thanks," Roxy said, "but I'm just looking for some information."

"About what?" The girl was young, smaller than Roxy, dark-haired and pretty.

"I heard that Lady Gunsmith was shot here."

"Oh, that," the girl said, making a face.

"Is it true?"

"Come on inside, honey," the girl said. "My name's Mandy. You want a drink? Maybe some coffee?"

"Coffee sounds good."

"Come on," Mandy said, backing away. "Most of the girls are still in bed—asleep, that is. Madam Rosie will be down any minute."

Mandy closed the door and showed Roxy into the sitting room, filled with overstuffed furniture, gold fixtures and brocade curtains.

"Have a seat," Mandy said. "I'll pour you some coffee. God, but you're beautiful."

"You're very pretty, too."

Mandy stopped short and studied at Roxy, who had no idea what had just occurred to her.

"I don't suppose you like girls?"

"Girls? You mean—" Roxy hoped she wasn't blushing.

"I mean, like, to go upstairs with?"

"Uh, no, sorry," she said, "I don't."

Mandy poured them coffee and brought it over to Roxy.

"Have you ever tried?" she asked. "I mean, we smell so good, and we're soft . . ."

"No, I've never tried," Roxy said.

"Okay, forget it," Mandy said. "I can see I'm makin' you uncomfortable." She sat in a chair opposite Roxy. "Whataya wanna know?"

"I want to know what happened," Roxy said. "Who shot her, when, where? All of it. I notice there's nobody in town, right now. They're all in the church."

"They're all a bunch of hypocrites," Mandy said. "They're in church tryin' to figure out how to make this tragedy work for them."

"Tragedy?"

"A woman was killed," Mandy said. "That's nothin' to celebrate."

"Does anybody else feel the way you do?"

"All of us here, do," she said. "We're women, after all. Those town women, they're as bad as the men."

"Was it a man who killed her?" Roxy asked.

"Oh yeah," Mandy said, "two pigs."

"Mandy!" a woman's voice rang out.

Both Roxy and Mandy looked at the doorway. A large woman stood there, wearing a robe and a frown. She didn't, however, look as if she had just woken up. She was wearing make-up, and her hair had been combed. Roxy noticed that her fingernails were long, and painted red and assumed this was Madam Rosie.

"What are you doin', girl?"

"I'm tryin' to convince this beautiful woman to come up-stairs with me," Mandy said, "but she ain't havin' it."

"I'm sorry, dear," the woman said to Roxy, "but we ain't open yet. That is, unless you're lookin' for a job?"

"Didn't I tell ya?" Mandy said.

"I can tell ya, you'd be real popular here, especially given what's happened" the woman said. "You look so much like that Lady Gunsmith who got herself killed the other day."

"Hey, that's right," Mandy said. "You do look like her, a lot."

"So I've been told," Roxy said. "I'm sorry, I'm not here for a job, just for some information. And everybody else in town seems to be in church."

"That's because they're a bunch of money hungry bas-tards," she said, in disgust.

"That's what I said!"

"Mandy, go get the other girls up."

"Yes, Ma'am." She stood and looked at Roxy. "Maybe I'll see you later?"

"Maybe," Roxy said, although she doubted it. She liked sex with men too much to go upstairs with pretty Mandy. But she did smell very good.

As Mandy left the room, the older woman said, "I'm Madam Rosie. You might as well come with me to my office. Bring your coffee."

Madam Rosie poured herself a cup from the pot in a corner, and then led the way from the sitting room to her office, across the hall.

Chapter Eight

In Madam Rosie's office was a desk with a chair behind him, plus an extra chair.

"Have a seat," she said, sitting behind her desk.

Roxy sat, holding her coffee cup in her lap.

"Ya gotta excuse me," Rosie said, "I just woke up."

"You don't look like you just woke up," Roxy told her.

"Don't kiss up to me, girl," Rosie said. "I know what I look like, that's why I don't come outta my room til I'm fixed up." She sipped some coffee, then put the cup down on the desk. "Okay, what kind of information are you lookin' for?"

"I told Mandy I want to know who shot Lady Gunsmith, where and how? The whole story."

"Why are you interested?" Rosie asked. "Just because you look like her?"

"No, Ma'am," Roxy said, "it's because I am her."

Rosie stared at Roxy for a few moments, expressionless, and then a smile appeared on her face.

"Yeah, you are," she said.

"I am," Roxy insisted.

"No," Rosie said, "I'm sayin' I believe you. You absolutely are Roxy Doyle."

"Well, thank you," she said. "I just came here from Sunset, where another Roxy Doyle was apparently shot, and there they didn't believe me."

"From what I've heard about you," Rosie said, "about your beauty—not even knowin' how you handle a gun—it's got to be you. The other girl, the one who got killed, didn't hold a candle to you."

"How was she killed?"

"In the street, in a gunfight with two men," Mandy said. "That's why everybody in town is so excited. It was a fair fight. We heard about the other girl in Sunset, and she was shot in the back. The mayor and the town council, here, they think havin' it happen in a so-called fair fight gives Telegraph the upper hand."

"So-called?"

"Two against one?" Rosie said. "That don't sound so fair to me, I don't care who the one is."

"And what happened to the two men who killed her?"

"They're still here," Rosie said. "Bein' treated like kings. The mayor said they should each get a hotel room, free of charge. And they ain't bein' charged for their meals, either."

"What about girls?" Roxy asked.

"If they're bein' given girls, they ain't comin' from here."

"That's good to know."

"It must be odd," Rosie said, "you seein' not one, but two of your own graves."

"Yes, very," Roxy said.

"So you wanna know who's behind it?"

"That's right."

"I can't help you with that," Rosie said. "All I know is, we here in this house didn't think it was somethin' to celebrate."

"Well," Roxy said, "that's something."

"Of course," she said, "you could work here while you're tryin' to find out. Under an assumed name, of course. Make some money while you're . . . investigatin'?"

Roxy smiled. "You mean make you some money, don't you? Because I look like a dead woman?"

Rosie shrugged. "It was just a thought."

"Sorry," Roxy said, "working in a bordello is just not something I see in my immediate future."

It was Rosie's turn to laugh.

"You think it was in any of our futures?" she asked.

Roxy stood up. "Thanks for the information."

"Just remember," Rosie said, "there's a place for you here any time you want."

"I'll keep that in mind."

Roxy left the office, saw several women coming down the stairs, in several modes of dress—or undress.

"Leavin'?"

She turned, saw Mandy just across the hall, at the door-way to the sitting room.

"Yes," Roxy said, "I have things to do."

"Did Madam tell you to come back anytime?"

"She did," Roxy said, "but I don't see it."

Mandy shrugged. "This wasn't what I wanted to do with my life, either. But . . ." She shrugged again. "I wish you luck, anyways."

"Thanks."

Mandy stepped forward and opened the door for Roxy. As she started to leave, the girl took hold of her arm.

"Come back and see me, though," she invited. "If you need a friend, I mean. Not . . ." She jerked her head toward the stairs.

"Thanks," Roxy said. "I might just do that, if I find I need a friend."

Mandy's smile broadened and she released Roxy's arm. As the redhead stepped outside, Mandy closed the door behind her, and she heard it lock.

Chapter Nine

There were people on the streets as she left the whore-house. Church must have let out. Some of them stared at her curiously, others just kept their eyes lowered.

She walked her horse to a livery stable and turned it over to a bored hostler who had nothing to say to her beyond "how long" and the price.

With her saddlebags and rifle, she walked from the livery to the nearest hotel. It didn't look like the biggest or best in town, but Roxy didn't need either. She just needed a room.

She stopped at the desk and dropped her saddlebags on it. "I need a room."

The clerk, in his mid-forties and tired looking, said, "For how long?"

"I'm not sure," she said. "Maybe a couple of days."

"Sign in."

She signed the register as "Mary Smith, as she had in Sunset. He held a key out to her and as she reached for it he snatched it back.

"Want some free advice with the room?"

"Sure," she said, "if you think I need it."

"You look a lot like Lady Gunsmith," he said, "who was killed here a couple of days ago. You might wanna do somethin' about that."

"Like what?" she asked. "Dye my hair, cut off my tits? Key, please."

He gave it to her and said, "It was just some friendly advice."

"Thanks."

She went to the stairs and up to the second floor. When she got to her room the door was already unlocked. Apparently, it was only the guests who locked them. She closed it behind her and followed suit.

The furniture was dusty, which suited her. It meant no one had been there in some time. She hated finding somebody else's fleas or bed bug in her hotel rooms. She dropped the saddlebags on the bed and walked to the window. It overlooked the front street, which was becoming even busier.

She unstrapped her gun and hung it on the bedpost, then went to the pitcher-and-basin on the dresser. She was surprised to find water there. It was tepid, but wet, so she washed with it. She let her hair down, shook it out, then put it back up and tied it, making sure it would stay under her hat, no matter what she encountered. Then she strapped the gun back on, and went out.

***

The saloons that had been locked earlier were now open, and doing a brisk business. It seemed that spending time in church was thirsty work.

The nearest saloon to Roxy's hotel was The Cactus. She went inside and, as usual, drew some looks from the men. She ignored them and walked to the bar.

"Beer," she told the bartender.

"Comin' up," the bartender said. He was a hard looking forty-year-old who didn't pay her any special attention at that moment. He drew the beer and set it down in front of her.

"Thanks."

"Sure."

As he started away she asked, "Got a minute?"

He stopped. "Sure. Whataya need?"

"Who's the law in this town?"

"Fella named Cotton Manning," the bartender said, "Sheriff Cotton Manning."

"Is he a good lawman?"

The bartender thought the question over. "He does his job."

"I heard somebody famous got killed here."

"You heard right. Lady Gunsmith, or so they say."

"What did the sheriff do about it?"

"Nothin'," the bartender said. "It was a fair fight, right out in the street."

"I heard it was two against one."

"You heard right."

"Doesn't sound so fair to me."

"Shoulda been," he replied, "if she was really Lady Gunsmith."

"You don't think she was?"

"No."

"Why not?"

"She's dead, ain't she?" he asked. "If she was who they say she was, they'd be dead."

"So she wasn't fast enough to be Lady Gunsmith?"

"Not nearly."

"How do you know that?"

He studied her for a moment, then said, "I've seen you before, a couple of years ago."

"That right?'

"It is."

"What's your name?"

"Jeff Wheeler," he said. "You don't know me."

She leaned forward.

"But you know me, right?"

"Right."

"Did you tell anybody else you didn't think it was her?"

"No," he said.

"And you heard about the woman in Sunset?"

"Oh yeah," he said, "but I knew that wasn't her—you—either."

"How'd you know that?"

"Same way," he said. "She was dead."

"You have a lot of faith in me."

"I saw you kill three men," he said, "outdrew them clean. You impressed me."

"Where was this?"

"In a town called Buffalo, Wyoming. It happened in the Occidental Hotel."

"That was three-and-a-half years ago," she said. "I remember. But I don't remember you."

"No reason you would."

First the older man in Sunset, and now this bartender. She'd been around the country long enough to start running into people who saw her in action.

"Thanks for the beer." She left half of it, reached for some money.

"On the house," he said.

"Thanks."

As she started to turn he said, "Somethin' you should know."

She turned back. "What's that?"

"You ever been to a town called Vinton?"

Chapter Ten

Vinton was only 5 miles from Telegraph, so she didn't even check out of her hotel. She went to the livery from the saloon, got her horse, and rode there. In the Vinton cemetery, the headstone read:

THIS HERE'S THE GRAVE OF
LADY GUNSMITH
SHOT TO DEATH IN VINTON

She stood there and stared at it in disbelief. Three headstones in three days, all announcing she was dead.

What the hell was going on?

The Vinton cemetery was small, not well cared for. Her grave was the freshest, the others overgrown with weeds. The town was also small and, according to the bartender, Jeff Wheeler, had no law. The story was she had been shot and killed in her hotel room. Vinton had one hotel.

She walked into the small town, leading her horse by its reins, right up to the little, run down hotel. A man was sitting on the front porch, whittling. He was in his 60's, thin as a rail and, standing, might have been five feet.

"You wanna room?"

"No."

"Whataya want, then?"

"I want to look at a room."

"Which one?"

"The one Lady Gunsmith was shot in."

He looked up from his whittling and smiled.

"Four bits a look," he said, "that's the goin' price."

The other two towns, Sunset and Telegraph, thought the shooting would make them famous. This town was charging four bits a look.

She gave it to him.

***

She entered the room and closed the door behind her. From the looks of it, it hadn't been cleaned since the occupant was killed. She looked around, but didn't find anything. Someone must have removed the woman's saddlebags, or whatever belongings she had.

In the center of the floor was a dried bloodstain. That was where the girl masquerading as her bled out.

Roxy walked to the window and looked out. She had a view over the front of the hotel, but there wasn't much happening on the street.

There was nothing in the room to help her. She was going to have to talk to the local sheriff, even though she'd heard nothing good about him.

She left the room and went back downstairs. No front desk, just the old man sitting out front, whittling.

"Find out anythin'?" he asked.

"No."

"They come and took her stuff."

42

"Who did?"

He shrugged. "Two men. I don't know who they was."

"But you let them go up?"

"Four bits is four bits."

"What was she like, the woman?"

"Pretty," he said, "but not like you. And she didn't talk much . . . not like you."

"Did you see the shooting?"

"Nobody saw the shootin'," he said. "it happened in the room."

"Was she shot in the back?"

The man shook his head.

"Right in the front, three times."

"Is there an undertaker in this town?"

"Nope."

"Then who buried her?" she asked. "Where did they take her?"

"They stuck her body in a barn, and then some fellers took her to Boot Hill and buried her."

"Who?"

"I didn't ask."

"What can you tell me about the sheriff here?"

"He ain't much," the man said, "but then, this ain't much of a town, is it?"

"You think that'll change now that she was killed here?" she asked.

He shook his head.

"Some people think so, but not me."

"Why not?"

"Because a nothin' town is a nothin' town," he said. "You wanna find out somethin' don't even bother with this place. Go to Sunset, or Telegraph, where the other ones was shot."

"You know about them?"

"Sure, don't you?"

"Are there anymore?" she asked. "Anymore killings, anymore graves?"

"Far as I know, just the three," he said, "but ain't that enough?"

"It's enough," Roxy said. "It's more than enough."

Chapter Eleven

Roxy rode back to Telegraph, the second town with her grave in it. After all, she still had a hotel room there. She put her animal up in the livery and walked to the hotel. After a ride to Vinton, the place was looking a little better to her.

She sat on the bed and thought about the events of the past few days. Did it really matter? She was alive, three women pretending to be her were dead. They probably got what they deserved. She was supposed to be trying to pick up her missing father's trail, not dealing with this nonsense.

But she had to admit to being curious. Why were these women pretending to be her? Why in these three towns so close to each other? And why now?

And who could she ask these questions of?

She decided there was no harm in spending a little time on this, but she wasn't going to get any answers sitting in her room. So she left it, and headed for the Cactus Saloon.

***

This late in the day the saloon was doing the business it should've been doing. Unlike when she rode into town and it was locked up.

The bartender, Jeff Wheeler, was busy behind the bar, but not too busy to notice her as she entered. He started waving his arms to make room at the bar, so that by the time she reached it, there was plenty.

"Back so soon?" he asked.

"Vinton wasn't much of a town," she said. "Can I have a beer?"

"Lady, you can have whatever you want."

Some of the men at the bar were staring at her, wondering what they were seeing.

Wheeler set the beer in front of her, and leaned on the bar.

"What'd you find out in Vinton?"

"Not much," she said. "There's no lawman there. Just an old guy sitting in front of the hotel where she was killed."

"Where you were killed, you mean?"

She looked around to see who had heard what he said.

"Oh, they're curious," he told her. "Another beautiful red-head in town. They're wonderin' if this place is really gonna be on the map because of that headstone on Boot Hill."

"Probably not," she said. "I'll have to come forward at some point."

"Yeah, but where?" Wheeler asked. "Here? Sunset?"

"That's going to take some thinking," she said. "Sunset would probably make more sense, since that's where my most recent demise took place."

"What about the two men in Vinton who gunned down the woman there?" Wheeler asked. "Did you see them?"

"I don't have to," she said. "I don't have to see them, or whoever killed the woman in Sunset, or whoever did it here. You know why?"

"Sure I do," Wheeler said. "because once you come forward and announce who you are, they'll probably be coming for you . . . again!"

"Only they won't find it as easy, this time," she said.

Wheeler looked around. His arm waving had cleared her a large part of the bar, even though it caused crowding at the rest of it. So no one had yet been able to hear what they were talking about.

"You wanna announce that right here and now?" he asked.

"No, not tonight," she said. "I'm a little tired. But I think tomorrow I'll be riding back to Sunset to talk to the law there, again. Maybe Sunset will end up on the map. I'll probably call out the killers of those three poor women who, for some reason of their own, were masquerading as me. Maybe they thought they were going to be treated a certain way. Free food, free drinks, free rooms. I don't know. What they got was free lead. But if the men who killed them want a shot at the real Lady Gunsmith, I just might oblige them in Sunset."

"Well," Wheeler said, "before you leave you might wanna have a talk with Sheriff Manning, here in Telegraph."

"Why's that?"

"He heard you were in town."

"From you?'

"Not me," Wheeler said. "I ain't said a word. Mighta been the desk clerk at the hotel."

"I'll have a talk with the clerk," she said, "and then maybe with the sheriff, before I leave. Thanks for the advice."

"Sure thing," Wheeler said.

"Maybe you have some more advice for me?" she asked.

"I might," he said. "I'd have to think about it."

"Well," she said, tossing a coin on the bar, "if anything occurs to you, I'll be in my room."

Wheeler studied her, wondering if this was some kind of invitation.

Roxy gave him a long look, trying to confirm her message. After the last couple of days she needed a stress reliever, and Jeff Wheeler looked like he might fit the bill.

"I'll do that," he said. "Yes, I will."

"Until later, then," she said, and walked out.

***

After she left, patrons at the bar closed rank, and the space she'd been standing in disappeared.

"Who was that?" a man named Blake asked.

"A new friend of mine," Wheeler said.

"She was pretty," another man, Jacob, said.

"You know who she reminded me of? She looks like—" Blake asked.

Wheeler cut him off by asking, "How about a drink on the house, boys?"

In that moment, Blake and Jacob just turned their attention to drinking.

***

The center of her back itched as she walked back to her hotel. One red haired woman had already been shot in the back, but she felt fairly safe, at the moment. She didn't think the word had gone out yet that she was there. The killers—whoever they were—were probably still celebrating the fact that they had killed Lady Gunsmith. She was going to get a good night's rest, as well as some welcome stress relief courtesy of Jeff Wheeler, and be ready to reveal herself the next day.

In her room she poured water into the basin and got herself cleaned up for the bartender, Wheeler. She'd been riding all day, and probably could have used a bath, but she had a feeling he was the kind of man who wanted a woman to smell like a woman, and not like soap.

Chapter Twelve

Roxy was reclining on the bed, her feet bare, but still dressed, when there was a knock on her door. It was sooner then she'd expected, as she thought Wheeler would have to close the saloon, first.

However, she'd heard too many knocks on her hotel room doors that turned out to be . . . disappointing. Rather than assume it was Wheeler she grabbed her gun from the holster hanging on the bedpost and carried it to the door with her.

"Who is it?"

"Jeff Wheeler. I, uh, think I was invited."

She opened the door a crack, saw that he was alone, and then opened it wide.

"Mr. Wheeler," she said, "yes, you were invited."

"Then can I come in?"

Roxy took the opportunity to look both ways in the hall, then backed away and said, "Come ahead."

As he entered he saw the gun in her hand.

"Occupational hazard?" he asked.

"Life hazard," she corrected. "That is, if I want to keep on living."

She walked to the bed and holstered the gun, then turned to face the bartender.

He walked right up to her and kissed her. She liked that. A lot of men started out intimidated by her. Kissing him back, she started to unbutton his shirt. He ran his hands down her back, pulled her shirttail out of her trousers, and slid his hands beneath it to touch bare flesh.

She peeled his shirt off and peppered his chest with kisses, enjoying the fact that he had not made an effort to wash, but had obviously come directly from the saloon. He smelled like a man.

He slid his hands down to her butt, lifted her off the floor and deposited her on the bed. As he tried to remove her trousers she kicked him away and slid off the mattress. Then she turned and pushed him down.

"Oh," he said, "you like to be in charge."

"I insist on it," she admitted.

She unbuckled his belt and peeled his pants and underwear down to his boots, which she removed. Then she tossed everything in a corner, leaving him entirely naked.

He was excited already, and his cock stood stiff and long, just the way she liked. She took it in one hand and stroked it, while reaching beneath his balls with the other. She was impressed when he grew even harder.

She released him, then, took a few steps back and proceeded to undress as he watched. When she was naked she stood with her hands on her hips while he took in the full breasts with their heavy, rounded undersides, her wide hips, and pale skin—except for her hands, which she couldn't hide from the sun. With her hat she was pretty much able to keep her face shielded. She always remembered how the sun wrinkled the face of the woman who had taken her in when her father went on the trail.

"My God," he said, "you're beautiful!"

She was impatient. She had no desire for any kind of fore-play, so she slid onto the bed with him, climbed aboard, and took his cock inside her wet pussy. Then she proceeded to ride him, looking for that stress reliever she needed, while he pawed and bit her bouncing breasts . . .

Normally, she would have sent him on his way when she was done with him, but she actually wasn't done, yet.

His hard cock was a pretty thing, and she wanted to spend some more time with it. So after a short rest for the two of them she slid down and pressed the hot column of flesh to her face, enjoying the feel of the smooth skin there. She hated men who had huge, veiny things between their legs. This pretty thing was so much better.

She rubbed it on her cheeks, and her lips, then stuck out her tongue and licked it, first from the bottom up on one side, then down on the other. When she had it good and wet she opened her mouth and took it inside, pausing to gently suck on the bulging head, then taking as much of the length inside as she could.

As she started to suck him he reached down to put his hands on her head. She immediately released him from her mouth—almost spitting him out—and snapped, "Don't do that!"

"Sorry," he said, quickly. "I didn't mean—"

"Keep your hands at your sides," she said. "You're going to enjoy this."

So he obeyed, put his hands at his sides, and she once again took him in her mouth to suck him. As she brought him to the brink he closed his fists, taking a handful of sheet in each, to quell the desire to reach for her head. He was afraid if he did it again, she'd stop for good.

Finally he couldn't stand it anymore and as he exploded into her mouth he let out a loud roar which confirmed what she had told him.

He enjoyed it.

***

"Lady," he said, moments later, "you sure know what you're doin'."

"It's easy to know what you men want," she said.

"And what about what you want?"

She yawned. "Oh, I got what I wanted. Don't worry. But now it's time for you to go."

"What?"

"It's time for me to get some sleep."

"And I can't stay?"

"I sleep alone," she said. "And how would you like it if somebody broke in here with guns blazing, and you got killed instead of me?"

"So you're kickin' me out for my own benefit?"

"Yeah," she said, "that's it."

She rolled over, didn't watch while he got dressed, again.

"Do I get at least a goodbye?" he asked.

"Why?" she asked. "I'm not your little woman."

She sensed that he was standing there, somewhat stumped at the treatment. But she'd gotten what she wanted and couldn't wait for him to leave. Rolling over to speak, or kiss him goodnight, would just keep him there longer. And in the position she was now in, her gun was well within reach, in case he got abusive.

But that didn't happen. The floor creaked as he finally moved, and she heard the door close. Only then did she roll over to make sure that he was gone.

And then she went to sleep.

Chapter Thirteen

Buffalo, Wyoming
3 ½ years earlier . . .

She was 21 when she rode into the small, sleepy town of Buffalo, Wyoming. The word she'd gotten about her father was that he was living there, and using the Occidental Hotel as a base of operations, still hunting bounty.

In the year and a half since she had trained with Clint Adams, her legend had grown slowly. While there were certain parts of the West—or, to be more precise, the Southwest— where she was known, there were more parts of the country where she wasn't. Wyoming was one of them. So when she rode into Buffalo the looks she drew were simply for being a beautiful red haired girl on a horse.

She reined in her horse in front of the Occidental, tied it there so it could drink from the trough, and went inside. She went directly to the front desk. There was another man in the lobby, dozing in a chair with his hat covering his eyes.

"I'm looking for a man named Gavin Doyle."

The grey-haired man behind the desk didn't react to the name, but studied her for a few moments.

"Why d'ya want him?" he asked.

"Is that important?" Roxy asked. "Does he live here?"

"He lives here," the man said. "Is this about work?"

Roxy decided to play it that way.

"Yes, it is."

"You're a little young to be a bounty hunter, ain'tcha?" he asked.

"I'm not a bounty hunter," she said, "he is, right?"

"Well, yeah."

"I'm here to offer him a bounty," she said. "What room is he in?"

"He's in five, but he ain't around, right now."

"Where is he?"

"He's on a job."

"When is he due back?"

"Tomorrow."

"Well then," she said, "I suppose I better have a room."

"Can you afford it?"

"If I'm here to offer him a job, don't you think I can afford a room?"

"Lemme see yer money, lady."

She took out a few coins and some paper money and showed it to him.

"All right," he said. "Sign in." He turned to get her a key from the wall.

She signed the register ROXANNE DOYLE. She didn't think the man would actually read it, and if he did it might not mean anything to him.

As it turned out, she was right. He turned the book back around and never glanced at it, simply handed her a key.

"Room ten," he said.

"Thank you. Where's the nearest livery stable?"

"Just down the street."

"I'll take care of my horse and come back."

"Whatever you like."

She left the hotel and walked her horse to the livery. While handing him over she asked the hostler, "Do you know Gavin Doyle?"

"Everybody around here knows Gavin," the man said. "He's livin' over at the Occidental."

"How long has he lived there?"

"A few months, I guess."

"Does he keep a horse here?"

"No, Ma'am, not here. There's another stable behind the Occidental."

She wondered why the clerk did not offer her that one?

"Do you know where I can find him?" she asked.

"Well," the man said, "when he's in town he's at the Occidental."

"I have a room there," she said, "so I guess I'll just wait."

"Are you in the same business he's in?"

"Sort of."

"Yer kind of young for a bounty hunter, ain'tcha?"

"Where can I get a good meal?" she asked, purposely ignoring his question.

"The Occidental has a good restaurant, and there's another one right across the street from it."

"Okay, thanks."

It looked like she was going to be stuck in town a while, just waiting . . .

After Roxy left the Occidental the clerk opened the register and looked at the name she had signed. It raised both his eyebrows. He came around the desk, went over to the dozing man and nudged his foot.

"Huh? What?" He pushed his hat up off his eyes and glared at the clerk.

"I got a message for you to deliver," the clerk said.

"To who?"

"Gavin Doyle," the clerk said, "and he needs to get it before he rides into town. You savvy?"

"I'm only a quarter Mexican," the younger man said, "but I savvy."

Chapter Fourteen

Roxy decided not to go back to the Occidental to eat, or claim her room, just yet. Instead, she stopped in at the restaurant across the street, which was called The Sagewood Café. It was her custom not to sit near a window, something she learned from Clint Adams, the Gunsmith, but she was pretty sure nobody in Buffalo knew who she was. Also, she wanted to be able to keep an eye on the front of the hotel.

So she broke with custom and got a seat at the window, set down her saddlebags and rifle, and ordered a bowl of beef stew and a cold beer. She kept watch out the window while she ate.

"You just get to town, honey?" the waitress asked, eyeing her saddlebags.

"That's right."

"You lookin' fer somebody in particular?" the middle-aged waitress asked.

"I am," she said, "A man."

"Ain't that always the way," the woman said, "He run off and leave ya?"

"Actually," she replied, "he did, but it's not what you think."

"Well, who is he?" the woman asked. "Maybe I know the bastard."

"His name's Gavin Doyle."

"Doyle?" the woman said. "I know him. Kind of a mean cuss, but then he hunts bounty for a livin', after all."

"That's him."

"You a bounty hunter, too?" the woman asked.

"No," Roxy said, "I just have some business with him."

"Well, you're in the right place, then," the waitress said. "He lives across the street, and takes a lot of his meals right here, or in the Winchester."

"Winchester?"

"A steakhouse down the street."

"Thanks."

"Sure thing," the woman said. "Yeah, I didn't think you was a bounty hunter."

"Why's that?"

"Too young," the waitress said, and walked away.

***

Roxy took her time with her meal. During that period the foot traffic out front was sparse, and she never saw her father—or anyone else, for that matter—enter the hotel.

When she was finished eating she paid her bill, thanked the waitress again, and crossed over to the hotel. When she went in the clerk watched her as she walked to the stairs and went up.

The room was small and clean, with a surprisingly comfortable mattress. The window looked down on the quiet front street, and there was no outside access to it from a balcony or low hanging roof, which suited her.

She decided that waiting in the room would be too boring, so now that she had taken a look at it, she left her saddlebags and rifle in a corner and went back downstairs. The Occidental had a dining room attached, and a saloon, but before she settled into that, she wanted to take a look at the town.

Down the street, as the waitress had told her, she saw the Winchester Steakhouse. Right across the street was the Cowboy Saloon, so she walked over to it and entered.

The hour was between lunch and supper, and the saloon was mostly empty. The men who were there lifted their heads long enough to look at her, then went back to their drinks. The bartender gave her a look, as did the single saloon girl working the floor. There was no gaming going on at the moment.

She walked to the bar and the bartender came over from the end of the bar, where he'd been talking with the girl.

"Beer, please," she said.

"Pleasure," he said.

While he got the beer the saloon girl moved down the bar to stand next to Roxy.

"Just get to town?" she asked.

"A little while ago," Roxy said. "I just ate in the Sage-brush."

"Good food, there," the girl said. She was young, maybe a year or two older than Roxy, but with creamy skin and clear blue eyes.

"Yes, it was."

The bartender brought Roxy her beer, looked at the saloon girl, who seemed to jerk her head at him. He walked back to the end of the bar. Roxy thought that the man's age was probably still higher than hers and the saloon girl's, combined.

"I'm Lacy," the girl said, sticking out her hand.

"Roxy." They shook hands.

"That's Gordo," the girl said, indicating the bartender. "Where are you stayin'?"

"The Occidental."

"Good choice," the girl said. "Nice rooms, comfortable beds."

"Guess I'll find out tonight, when I go to sleep," Roxy said.

"Yeah," Lacy said, "or you could find out sooner."

Roxy studied the girl a moment, and it took that moment for her to realize what the girl was offering.

"Or," Lacy said, making it even clearer, "we could go to my room."

Chapter Fifteen

"You're a lovely girl," Roxy said, "but I'm really not interested."

"You can't blame me for tryin'," Lacy said. "You're beautiful."

"Well . . . thank you," Roxy said. "I appreciate the compliment."

"If you should happen to change your mind," Lacy said, "I'll be here."

"I'll remember."

The girl reached and lightly brushed Roxy's cheek, then lowered her hand.

"Beautiful," she said again, then turned and went back to her position at the bar.

Roxy studied the room while she worked on her beer. The men in the place looked like either merchants, or ranch hands. And they all seemed to be very interested in what they were drinking.

She finished the beer, called the bartender back and settled up.

"Sure you don't wanna go upstairs with Lacy?" Gordo asked.

All of Roxy's sexual experience to that point in her life had been with men, and very little of it enjoyable. It was forced on her early, but she also learned to use it to her advantage early. The times that she'd had sex for the sheer enjoyment of it could be counted on the fingers of one hand. Normally, she used it as a way to control men. Having sex with a woman had just never occurred to her. Sure they were pretty, and smelled good, but that was an experience that would have to wait for some time in the future—if ever.

"I'm sure," she told him.

"Pity," Gordo said.

"No offense," Roxy said.

"None taken sweetie," Lacy called from her end of the bar.

Roxy knew the girl, though only a year or two older, was infinitely more experienced than she was. She didn't know what else to do, so she just turned and left the saloon, feeling intimidated.

Lacy smiled at Gordo and said, "She'll be back . . ."

***

Outside the Cowboy, Roxy felt slightly foolish for being thrown off balance by the boldness of Lacy. She wondered if, back inside, they were laughing at her? Not that it really mattered.

At least she had enough information about her father to believe he actually was in Buffalo. All she had to do was wait for him to come back. But where to wait, that was the question. She decided that since he lived in the Occidental, and she had a room there, she might as well wait in the hotel.

There were several wooden chairs out front, so she dragged one over and plopped herself down in it. The word from the clerk was that her father would be returning tomorrow, but if he got back early she didn't want to miss him.

***

Several hours later, while she was still sitting there, three riders came down the street, not in any hurry. She knew the look of them, though. They weren't cowboys, they were hunters. She could tell the way their eyes took everything in, while not seeming to.

As they passed, they looked her over, and she looked right back. Almost as an afterthought, the lead rider swerved over to her, and reined in his horse in front of the hotel—and her.

"You live here, girl?" he asked.

"I don't," she said, "and don't call me girl."

He looked to be in his late twenties, maybe even younger as he snatched his hat off his head and held it over his heart.

"Oh, I'm sorry, Ma'am," he said, sarcastically. "I didn't mean to offend."

His two partners rode up alongside him, and she thought she knew what was coming.

"Even if you don't live here," the first man asked, "would you happen to know if Gavin Doyle does?"

"Who wants to know?" she asked.

"We do, Ma'am," he said. "My name's Dan Holman. This here's Al Boyd, and that's Rick Wheeler."

"What do you want with Doyle?"

65

"Well," Holman said, "not that it's any of your business, but it's him who wants somethin' of us. See, he's a bounty hunter, and he's lookin' for us."

"Then why are you here?" she asked. "Why ain't you running?"

"Well," he said, "runnin' just ain't in my blood. So we thought we'd make it real easy for him to find us."

"As far as I know, he ain't in town." That much was true.

"I guess since the word we got was that he lives here at the Occidental, I guess we'll just dismount and have a drink while we wait."

"I don't think that'd be such a good idea," she told him.

"Is that a fact?" he said. "Well, I don't recall askin' you for your opinion on that." he put his hat back on. "Ma'am!" he looked at his two companions. "Come on, boys, let's get a drink."

They dismounted, tied their horses, and went inside the Occidental Saloon.

Chapter Sixteen

Roxy was concerned about her father.

If the three men had been looking for Clint Adams, she wouldn't have moved from her chair. The Gunsmith could handle three such men with no difficulty. In fact, she thought that she could handle them, as well. She'd become very proficient with her gun since the Gunsmith took her under his wing.

But Gavin Doyle had a reputation as a deadly man tracker, not a gunfighter. Facing three men in the street didn't sound like his ideal situation. She, however, had already done it several times, successfully, which was why she was already known in some parts of the county as Lady Gunsmith.

But what to do about it was not immediately evident to her. Call the three men out and face them herself before her father got back? How would she explain that to the lawman in town? On the other hand, she could go inside the saloon, make nice and drink with the three men, perhaps even take the leader to bed. Convince him to take his friends and leave town.

She decided that, before she could do anything, she had to get out of that chair.

***

In the saloon, Holman, Boyd and Wheeler bellied up to the bar and ordered beers.

"This might not be such a bad town," Holman said to his partners.

"You mean because of that girl?" Boyd asked.

"That's exactly what I mean."

The three men were roughly the same age, but while Holman's main interest in life seemed to be women, Boyd and Wheeler were more concerned with money—and staying alive.

"I think you should have your mind on Doyle, Dan," Wheeler said, "not some girl."

"Yeah, but you saw her," Holman said. "That wasn't just some girl that was some girl."

Both men knew if they didn't need Holman's gun, they'd cut him loose. The only reason they rode with him at all was because he helped them stay alive. He figured to be the one who was going to gun down Gavin Doyle. They were just there to back his play.

"Keep your mind on your work until after the deed is done," Boyd said. "Then you can go after the girl."

"Well," Holman said, "before that happens, we've got to find Doyle."

"The word is he lives here," Wheeler said. "If we stay around here, don't worry, we'll find him."

The three men drank their beers.

***

Roxy found the sheriff's office. Inside she found a man with a badge, playing solitaire at his desk. He was concentrating very hard.

"Sheriff?"

"That's me." He had a deep voice, which belied his slight frame. She figured him for his mid-forties, which might explain why he thought playing solitaire on the job was the right thing to do. He'd probably been a lawman for a long time.

"I rode into town today looking for Gavin Doyle," she said.

"I heard that."

"Well, three men just rode in looking for him too," she said. "They're over at the Occidental Saloon."

For the first time since she entered the office he looked up from his game. When he saw her, he put the deck of cards he was holding down.

"Well, look at you," he said, and did just that.

"Did you hear what I said?" she asked. "Three men are looking for Doyle."

"I heard you," he said. "I didn't know that, but now I do. Thanks."

"Well, what are you gonna do about it?"

"Do?" he asked. "What would you like me to do, little lady?"

She let the "little lady" go.

"They're looking to kill him because he's hunting them," she explained.

"They told you this?"

69

"Well, no," she said. "I mean, the hunting part, yeah. And they said they thought they'd make it easy for him to find them."

"I'm sure Doyle will appreciate that."

"Three against one, Sheriff," she said. "Doesn't that concern you?"

He sat back in his chair and looked at her anew. "Say, what's your interest in Doyle? You wouldn't be lookin' to kill him, too, wouldja?"

"If I was," she said, "would I be telling you about these three men?"

"Maybe you want me to toss them in a cell and leave a clear field for you," he offered.

"I don't want to kill Gavin Doyle," she said.

"Then why do you want him?" he asked. "What's your business with him?"

She tightened her lips, then said to the lawman, "I'm his daughter."

Chapter Seventeen

"I didn't know Doyle had a daughter," the sheriff said.

"Well, he does," she said. "He left me years ago, after my mother was killed."

"And you don't wanna kill him?"

"He left me with some people so he could go off and make money," she said. "How was he to know they'd . . . never mind. No, I don't want to kill him. I just want to find him. Which means I don't want the three men to kill him, either."

"Miss . . . Doyle, is it?"

"Roxy Doyle."

"Miss Doyle, I'm sure your father can handle three men he's huntin'. If not, he wouldn't be huntin' them, would he?"

"But he's not in town," she said, "and won't be until to-morrow. If he rides in and doesn't know they're here—"

"All right," he said, stealing a glance back at his cards. Perhaps he wanted her to leave so he could pick up the deck and resume the game. "Suppose he does know they're here?"

"How's he going to know that?"

"Well, one of us will have to tell 'im, that's all. Watch for when he gets back, get to him first, and warn him. How's that?"

"I was thinking along the lines of making them leave town," she offered.

"And how do you propose we do that?" he asked.

"Sheriff, what's your name?"

"Baker," the lawman said, "Sheriff Larry Baker." And now he did pick up the deck of cards and resume his solitaire game, frowning with concentration.

"It seems to me you're a little more interested in your solitaire than you are in saving a man's life."

"This is a game of skill, you know," he told her. "You have to pay special attention to the suits—"

"Never mind," she said. "I'll take care of the situation, myself."

"Take care of it yourself?" he asked, looking up at her again. "Just what does that mean?"

"I guess you'll have to wait and find out," she said. "Black Queen on Red King."

He looked down at the cards on his desk. "Oh yeah, thanks."

She slammed the door on her way out.

***

When she got to the Occidental the three men were standing at the bar. Instead of going in, she entered the hotel lobby and went to the desk.

"Can I help ya?" the clerk asked.

"Yes, the three men at the bar, who just rode in?"

"I'm not sure who you mean."

"Then go and have a look," she said. "I'll wait."

He came around from behind the desk, walked to the doorway of the saloon and looked inside. He waited several moments, then came back.

"See them?" she asked.

"I seen them," he said. "So?"

"Did they talk to you?"

"About what?"

"Gavin Doyle."

The man hesitated, then said. "The only person who has talked to me about Doyle today is you."

So they didn't need to confirm that Doyle lived there. They actually knew that when they rode in.

"Are you sure Doyle will be back tomorrow?" she asked. "I'm sure."

"No chance he'll get back today?"

"None."

"Okay, well they're looking for him."

"So are you."

"Not for the same reasons."

"How do I know that?"

"Because I'm telling you, right now," she said. "They told me he's hunting them, so they're making it easy for him to find them."

The clerk stared at her for a few seconds, then said, "Hmph. Okay, that don't sound good."

"No, it don't," she said.

"What do you want me to do about it?"

"Warn him."

"How?"

"The same way you already warned him about me." She turned and looked at the chair the man had been sitting in, which was now empty.

"I didn't—"

"Don't lie to me," she said. "It's not going to help the situation."

He shrugged, and didn't say anything.

"I'm going in the saloon now," she said. "If you hear shooting, send for the sheriff."

"Yes, Ma'am."

She nodded, turned and went into the saloon.

Chapter Eighteen

As she entered the saloon she drew the attention she normally did, but her concentration was on the three men at the bar. They were drinking and laughing as if they had no cares in the world.

"You three at the bar!" she said, loudly.

It got quiet all of a sudden. Not only the three men, but everyone else in the saloon fell silent and turned to look at her.

"Are you talkin' to us?" Holman asked.

"I am," she said, again. "I don't think you understood what I was saying outside."

"I think we got the point," Holman said. "You were suggesting that we run because Gavin Doyle's huntin' us? Do I have that right?"

"You got it," she said.

"It's not gonna happen, girlie," he said, "so you might as well go buy a hat, or dress, or somethin'. And leave us be. We got some drinkin' to do."

"No, you don't," Roxy said. "You're leaving, not just the saloon, but town."

"Is that a fact?" Holman looked at his friends, who grinned at him. "And who's gonna make us leave?"

"I am."

"And why would you wanna do that, little girl?" Holman asked.

"Because I'm not a little girl," she said. "I'm Gavin Doyle's daughter."

That drew a murmur from the others who were watching. The three men, though, didn't seem that concerned with it.

"Look," Holman said, "you're gonna get yourself hurt, sweetie—"

"I'm not your sweetie, or baby, and I'm not a little girl," she said. "I'm going to give you until the count of three to get on your horses and ride out of town."

"The count of three?" he asked. "That hardly seems fair. I don't think we could get to the door in a count of three." He and his friends laughed.

But rather than be thrown by the remark, Roxy said to him, "Try."

That made the smile fade from not only Holman's face, but the faces of Boyd and Wheeler, as well.

"Yer pushin' yer luck," Wheeler said.

"Yeah," Boyd agreed, "maybe we ain't gonna be so nice, anymore."

Lacy, the saloon girl, was watching the action at the end of the bar, her nostrils flaring and her breasts heaving with excitement. Roxy thought it was odd that, in that moment, she noticed how very pretty the girl was. Maybe if she'd gone upstairs with the girl she wouldn't be standing here right now, facing three guns.

The men all got serious, put down their drinks and turned to face her, head on.

"Hey," the bartender complained, "you ain't gonna draw on a girl, are ya?"

"She's callin' the play," Holman said. "Besides, you heard 'er. She ain't a girl; she's Gavin Doyle's daughter."

"I'm giving the three of you one more chance to move on," Roxy said. "I want everybody here to witness that."

"Yeah, yeah," Holman said, "everybody knows it."

There was sudden movement in the room as everyone got up and moved out of range, especially the bartender, who fled from behind the bar.

"Anytime . . . girlie," Holman said.

She had her eyes on him. He was the first one she would kill, because he seemed to be the leader.

"Come on, come on!" Wheeler snapped at her.

"Take it easy, Wheel—" Holman started, but he was too late. He wanted Roxy to move first, but it was Wheeler who grabbed for his gun.

"Damnit!" Holman said.

Roxy drew. Before Holman could even decide to go for his gun, a bullet struck him square in the chest.

She turned her gun on Boyd next, because Wheeler had already fired and missed. He was just in too much of a hurry.

A bullet punched into Boyd, bouncing him off the bar before he hit the floor.

Wheeler fired again wildly, and Roxy calmly put a hole in his chest, ending his futility.

And then it was very silent in the bar, as most of the men couldn't believe what they had just seen.

Chapter Nineteen

Word got around town fast that Gavin Doyle's daughter had cleanly out drawn and killed three men.

She left the saloon immediately after, stopping only to eject her spent cartridges and reload. She walked over to the chair in front of the hotel and sat down to wait . . .

After about an hour Sheriff Baker appeared across the street. He looked over at her, then shook his head and walked her way.

"You made a helluva mess," he said.

"Not so much," she said. She had seen him direct several men to carry the bodies to the undertaker. He hadn't stopped by her first, but was now returning from the undertaker. "You put down your cards and cleaned it up."

"Yeah, I did," he said, "and I checked my posters. There was a bounty on each one of them, and you're entitled."

"Give it to my dad when he rides in tomorrow."

"You don't want the money?"

"I don't," she said. "Give it all to him."

"It's two hundred each."

"Good," she said, "he'll like that."

"You just gonna sit there and wait for him?"

"Except for when I eat, or go to bed," she said, "but I'll be back out here in the morning."

"And then maybe you'll both leave town, huh?" he asked. "Before somebody else gets killed?"

"That would suit me," she said.

"Yeah," he said, "it would suit a lot of people."

***

As promised, she had left the chair only to eat supper, and then go to bed. Early the next morning, after breakfast, she was back out in the chair, waiting.

She was sitting there in the afternoon when a lone rider came into town, riding slowly. She sat forward in her chair and narrowed her eyes, trying to get a good look at him. Finally, as he came close to the hotel, he turned his head and looked right at her, then continued on. He was riding as big grey with a white tail.

Roxy got up and went inside the hotel, to the desk.

"What kind of horse is Doyle riding?" she asked.

"Huh? Uh, his horse is grey, with a white tail."

She walked over to the chair where the man was once again dozing, as he had been when she arrived the day before.

"Huh? Wha—" he came awake, wide-eyed as she kicked his feet.

"Did you warn Gavin Doyle I was looking for him?"

He looked at the clerk, and then back to her.

"I sent a telegram," he said. "I dunno if he got it."

She turned and looked around the lobby. There was another chair across from the one the man was sitting in. She went over to sit down and wait.

About ten minutes later she heard the footsteps on the boardwalk, and then the man walked in. He looked at her again, and at the man who was usually dozing.

"Whatayou doin' awake?" he asked.

The man didn't answer.

The man, easily in his 40's, walked to the desk and asked, "Any messages for me?"

"Uh, well, yeah, Mr. Doyle, but . . ."

"Spit it out, I ain't got all day!"

"There's somebody waitin' to see ya."

"Who?"

"That girl."

The man claiming to be Gavin Doyle turned and looked at her again, frowning. Then he walked over to her.

"I know you?"

She stood up.

"No," she said, "you don't know me, and I don't know you."

"Then why are you lookin' for me?"

"I'm not," she said. "I was looking for Gavin Doyle."

"I'm Gavin Doyle," he told her. "Whataya want?"

"You ain't Gavin Doyle," she said, "because I'm Doyle's daughter, and you ain't him."

"Now look—"

She drew her gun quickly and pointed it at him. This was something the Gunsmith told her never to do. Never draw unless you're going to use it. But she wanted to make a point, here.

This man was wearing a gun, but carrying his saddlebags and rifle. He had no chance to make a move.

"Now wait—" he said.

"I want you to tell these two fellas and me your real name," she said.

"I just said—"

"If you say Gavin Doyle" she said, "I'm going to kill you."

He licked his lips, as sweat dripped down his face.

"Okay, wait," he said. "If you're Doyle's daughter and you wanna kill him, then you don't want me."

"Why not?"

"Becuz I ain't Doyle," he said.

"What's your name?"

"Ben Cutler."

"Why are you claiming to be Gavin Doyle?"

He shrugged. "Well, he's been missin', probably dead, and I didn't think there'd be no harm—"

"Oh, there's harm," she said. "There's definitely harm."

"Look, Miss," he said, "I'm sorry, I was just tryin' ta, you know, be somebody, and make some money."

She cocked back the hammer of her gun and pointed it right at his face.

"Jesus!" he squeaked, dropping his rifle and saddlebags to the floor and putting his hands up.

"Go and be somebody somewhere else," she told him. "And if I ever hear you're pretending to be Gavin Doyle again—"

"No, no," he said, "I swear, I won't!"

"Get out!" she snapped. "Out of town!"

"Y-yes, Ma'am."

He hurriedly picked up his rifle and saddlebags and ran out the hotel door, almost knocking the sheriff over.

The lawman approached Roxy as she holstered her gun.

"We all believed him," he said.

"Yeah," she said, "I guess a lot of people did."

"Are you sure—"

"I know what my father looks like," she said, "even after all these years."

"Well . . . what now?"

"Now you get what you want," she said. "No more Gavin Doyle in your town, and no more me."

"Look," he said, "if you wanna stay—"

"I don't," she said. "I'm just gonna give him time to saddle up and ride out, and then I'm heading for the livery to do the same."

"And do what?"

"Just keep looking," she said. "That's all I can do."

Chapter Twenty

She woke early the next morning, feeling refreshed from both the sex, and the sleep. When she had sex it wasn't always something wanted, but it was usually what she needed. And last night she had needed it.

But the sex had more than satisfied her physically. It had enabled her to sleep soundly, and because of that her mind relaxed, and memories of Buffalo, Wyoming came rushing back.

She killed three men there, thinking she was saving her father. She remembered their names.

Holman.

Boyd.

And Wheeler.

Wheeler, the same last name as the bartender she'd slept with, Jeff Wheeler.

The man who said he remembered her from Buffalo, only she didn't remember ever meeting him, or even seeing him, then. Of course, the name Wheeler could be a coincidence, but not after he claimed to have seen her kill three men in Buffalo, Wyoming, in the Occidental Saloon. Clint Adams had once told her there were no coincidences. She didn't know if she believed that or not, but in this case, it would be a stretch.

If the bartender was related to the man named Wheeler who she had killed 3 ½ years ago, then he could very well be involved with these phony Roxy Doyles who were killed. The question would then be, why hadn't he tried anything last night, when they were having sex and she might have been her most vulnerable?

The only way she was going to get the answers to that question, as well as a few more she could think of, was to find him, and ask.

She decided to have breakfast, and then stroll over to the Cactus Saloon and see what she could find out about Jeff Wheeler.

She didn't want to rush up on Wheeler so that he'd have an inkling that, maybe, she'd remembered something. After she finished her breakfast she calmly walked over to the saloon and banged her fist on the locked front door. If it was like every other saloon she'd ever been to, somebody was in there now, cleaning up and getting it ready to open. She could hear the sound of a broom sweeping.

She kept banging until somebody yelled, "Awright, awright, goddamnit!" and unlocked the door. It opened about a foot and a fat-faced man asked, "What the hell ya want? We're closed. I'm cleanin' the place up."

"Is Wheeler in there?" she asked. "Jeff Wheeler?"

"The bartender. No, just me. I'm the swamper, and yer interruptin' me."

"Do you know where he lives?"

"No. I don't know where nobody lives. I don't know who you are. And you know what? I don't wanna."

84

"Who owns this place?" she asked. "You've got to know that."

"Mr. Fletcher."

"And where can I find him?"

"The Carlyle Hotel."

"What room?"

"The biggest room," the swamper said. "He owns that place, too."

"Okay, thanks."

The swamper slammed the door and she could hear that he immediately went back to his sweeping.

***

The Carlyle was not hard to find, since it was the largest hotel in town. The lobby had several people in it, a man seated, reading a newspaper, a man and a woman apparently arguing over the amount of luggage one of them had, a spinsterish woman, standing off to one side, tapping her foot, probably waiting for someone. They all stopped to look at Roxy as she walked up to the desk, even the woman who was arguing with her husband couldn't help but stare.

"Yes, Ma'am?" the clerk asked. He was a well-dressed, slightly built man in his mid-thirties, who didn't seem particularly interested in how Roxy looked, only what she wanted.

"I'd like to see Mr. Fletcher."

"The owner?"

"That's right."

"Well . . . he's in his room—"

"Good," she said, heading for the stairs. "Largest room in the hotel, I assume it's on the top floor."

"Miss, you can't . . ." But she was already on her way up the stairs and didn't hear the rest of what the clerk had to say.

She had to go up two flights, to the third floor, and when she got there she realized that Fletcher's room might just possibly take up the entire level.

She found a door that looked like it could be the main door, and knocked, just as the clerk got to the level and, breathlessly, joined her.

"Now, Miss, I told you—" he started, but the door opened and interrupted him.

The man standing there was tall, broad shouldered, with a carefully trimmed mustache and dark hair shot with silver. He was wearing the trousers and vest that were part of an expensive suit.

"David, what's going on?" he asked, but he was looking at Roxy.

"This lady wanted to see you, and just barged up here—"

"Who's watching the desk while you're up here?"

"Well," the clerk said, "nobody—"

"Then you better get back down there," the man said. "I'll take care of the lady."

"But Mr. Fletcher—"

"Go!"

"Yessir."

The clerk turned and hurried back down the hall to the stairs.

"Do you have a name?" the man asked her.

"I do," she said. "Roxy."

"Well, Roxy, come on in and tell me what I can do for you."

Chapter Twenty-One

"This is quite a room," she said.

"It's a suite," he corrected her.

"A big hotel for a little town."

"After what's happened here, this town's going to get bigger," he replied, "and I'm going to be ready to take advantage of that growth. When people start coming here to see where Lady Gunsmith met her maker, they're going to need rooms. Now, just why is it you're looking for me? Do you want a job?"

"A job?"

"Yes," he said, "here in the hotel? Or my saloon? We take you out of those clothes and put you in a dress, you'd do very well at the saloon."

"Not interested," she said. "I'm looking for your bartender, Jeff Wheeler."

"Wheeler? Why would you be looking for him? He's a drifter, a nothing. I gave him a job last week, and he threw it in my face this morning."

"This morning?" she asked. "He quit?"

"That's right."

"And you only hired him last week."

"That's what I said." He seemed to be growing impatient with the subject.

"Is he still in town?"

"I don't know," he said, "I don't keep track of people who don't work for me."

"Well, when he was working for you did you know where he lived?"

"Is that really why you came here?" he said. "To ask me about him?"

"Why else did you think?"

"Well," he said, "I thought you may have heard something about me—"

"Look, Mr. Fletcher, I'm sure you're a very interesting man, but I just don't have the time, right now. I've got to find Jeff Wheeler."

"He had a room in the Baxter Hotel. Maybe he's still there."

"Thanks."

She headed for the door.

"Wait a minute," he said. "You haven't even told me who you are. Just that your name is Roxy—Roxy?" He stopped, realizing something wasn't right.

"That's right," she said, "Roxy Doyle. And I wouldn't count on that growth you were talking about."

She left him standing there with his mouth open.

***

Roxy found the Baxter Hotel. It was probably the most rundown building she'd seen in town, so far, located on a side street. As she stepped up to enter, she felt the boards beneath her feet were loose.

89

The lobby was empty, and hardly large enough to be called a lobby. She reached the front desk, but didn't dare touch it for fear it would fall apart. The clerk behind it looked at her with wide, watery eyes, and there was an odd smell coming either from him, or something else behind the desk. His age was difficult to gauge, but he wasn't young.

He scratched an armpit and asked, "Yeah?"

"Jeff Wheeler. What room is he in?"

"He ain't in any room." He switched sides, scratched the other pit. "He checked out."

"When?"

"This mornin'."

"Did he say where he was going?"

"Nah!" Now he vigorously scratched both armpits. Roxy backed away, afraid he might have fleas.

Did she want to bother checking Wheeler's room? There might be fleas there, as well. But she was there, and might as well . . .

"What room was his?"

"Three," the man said, "top of the stairs."

"Thanks."

"Uh-uh," he grunted, as she turned for the stairs. "Not for free."

She took out a coin and tossed it to him. He stopped scratching long enough to catch it. She went up the stairs, feeling they were loose, as well.

She made her way to room 3. The door was wide open. Inside the bed was a mess. He'd obviously went back there and slept in it, and then checked out come morning. She looked in the dresser drawers, found them empty. There was nothing in the room to give a clue where he might have gone, or who he really was.

If he had anything to do with the three dead "Roxy Doyles," why would he leave just when the real one arrived?

The answer?

He wouldn't.

If he wasn't in Telegraph he sure as hell wouldn't go to Vinton. There was nothing there. It was a mudhole in the road. That only left Sunset, and she had intended to go back there, anyway. It's where the last killing had taken place.

Or what she hoped was the last.

Chapter Twenty-Two

It was evening when Roxy rode into Sunset. The stores were closed, but the saloons were operating, and the noise from them was audible on the street.

Instead of going to one of the saloons—where she might have or might not have found Jeff Wheeler—she went to the sheriff's office. Jack Taggert looked up from his desk as she entered, and frowned.

"You're back."

"That's right, I'm back," she said. "I'm here to find out who killed three phony Roxy Doyle's, Sheriff."

"Did you bring me any proof that you're the real Roxy Doyle?"

"I don't have to prove that to anyone," she said. "I'll just do what I came to do and be on my way."

"Okay," Taggert said, "and just what is it you came to do?"

"Find a man named Jeff Wheeler."

"Who's he?"

"He was a bartender in Telegraph, at the Cactus Saloon."

"That's Tom Fletcher's place."

"Right. And Fletcher told me Wheeler quit and left town. I figure he came here."

"Why" And why are you interested in him?"

"Wheeler told me he knew about the phony in Telegraph because he had seen me before."

"He can identify you as Lady Gunsmith?"

"Yeah, he can," she said. "He saw me kill three men three-and-a-half years ago in Buffalo, Wyoming."

"Then I'd like to talk to him, too," Taggert said. "Why did he leave Telegraph so abruptly?"

"That's what I want to find out."

"You think he knows somethin' about all these phony Lady Gunsmiths?"

"So now you believe they were phony?"

"Well," Taggert said, "there were three of them, so at least two had to be phonies. I have your word for the fact that they were all phonies, and you're the real one. So, if I can get somebody else to support your story, I'd like to find him myself."

"So you don't know him?"

"I never heard of him until right now," Taggert said, "but I'm gonna find him. But just because he knows who you are doesn't mean he's involved in the whole mess. What makes you think that?"

"Because one of the men I killed that time in Buffalo was named Wheeler."

"So they're related?"

"That's what I want to find out."

"Okay, so why do you think he's here, in Sunset?" Taggert asked.

"Because this is the place the third and, I hope, the last woman was killed," Roxy told him. "For me, this is where it started."

"So then you won't ge goin' anywhere until you can find him?"

"I'll be here until I get the answers I want," she told him. "All the answers."

Taggert sat back in his chair, rubbed his jaw.

"You know, I'm startin' to believe you are actually Lady Gunsmith."

"That doesn't really matter much to me, Sheriff," she told him.

Roxy turned and started to leave.

"Where are you goin', now?"

She turned to look at him.

"To take care of my horse," she replied, "get a hotel room, and start looking for Jeff Wheeler."

Chapter Twenty-Three

After she left the sheriff's office Roxy went directly to a livery stable and had her horse taken care of. What kind of hotel room she got didn't matter, so she just stopped at the first one she saw, got the room and left her saddlebags and rifle. Then she took to the street.

There were four saloons in Sunset. Roxy had a beer at each one. The last one she went to was the largest, the Live Oak. The sign announcing that Lady Gunsmith had her last drink there was still up. Roxy decided not to make a fuss about it. Not yet, anyway.

She stopped at the bar, ordered her fourth beer and asked the bartender to stay a moment.

"What can I do for you?"

"I'm thinking bartenders know bartenders, am I right?" she asked.

"Usually." He was a big man, with a deep chest and sloping shoulders. He leaned forward. "Who are you lookin' for?"

"A man named Jeff Wheeler," she said. "He worked at the Cactus in Telegraph."

"Worked?"

"He left."

"How long was he there?"

"Just about a week."

He shook his head. "I wouldn't have known him, then. I haven't been to Telegraph in months."

"He might be passing through, looking for work," she said.

"Well, he hasn't been here lookin' for a job," the man assured her.

"If he does show up, I'm at the Comstock Hotel. Please let me know."

"Sure," he said. "What's your name?"

She hesitated, then said, "Roxanne."

"Roxanne," he repeated. "I'm Bellamy." He put out his big hand.

She shook it. "Hello, Bellamy."

"Have you checked with the other saloons?"

"I looked," she said. "I didn't ask, though."

"If word gets around that you're askin' about him, he'll hear," Bellamy said. "Then you'll never find him, if he doesn't want you to."

"I suppose not."

"I mean," Bellamy said, "I don't know him, but if it was me, you wouldn't find me."

"I get it."

"You talk to the sheriff?"

"Yes," she said, "he's looking, too."

"Then if he's in town, he can't hide from you forever," Bellamy said. "And why would any man want to hide from you, anyway?"

She didn't answer.

"You're not gonna kill 'im, are you?"

"No," she said, "that's not why I'm looking for him."

"Then what is it?" Bellamy asked, laughing. "Are you in love with him?"

She made a face. "Hardly. He just knows something I need to know."

"So you have a question for him."

"Questions," she said, "I have questions for him. And I have a question for you?"

"What is it?"

She pushed her empty mug toward him.

"Can I have another beer?"

Chapter Twenty-Four

Roxy spent the rest of the night in the Live Oak, nursing her drinks so she wouldn't get too drunk. Despite that, she was starting to feel lightheaded. Then it occurred to her where Wheeler might have gone.

"Another one?" Bellamy asked.

"No," she said, "I've had enough. Good-night."

"'night."

She left the saloon, walked through the darkened streets to another building and knocked on the door.

"Well," Madam Rosie said, "look who's back. Come to see Mandy?"

"I'm looking for a man," Roxy said.

"Then you're in the wrong place," Madam said. "We don't offer that service, here."

"I'm looking for a man who might be with one of your girls," Roxy said.

"Ah," Madam Rosie said. "All right, you'd better come in."

Roxy entered and Madam closed the door and locked it.

"Come," she said, and led Roxy to the sitting room.

The room was filled with scantily clad girls and men of all size and ages, silly looks on their faces. There was no sign of Wheeler.

"He's not here," she said. "I'd like to look upstairs."

"You can't go upstairs," Madam Rosie said, "without a girl."

"All right."

"Pick one," Madam said.

"You pick for me."

"How about me?"

They both turned, saw that Mandy had just come into the room.

"Are you finished with Mr. Deming already?" Madam asked the young girl.

"He just wanted me to watch," Mandy said. "I didn't even get my hands dirty."

"All right, then." Madam Rosie turned back to Roxy. "Mandy will take you up."

Mandy smiled and put her hand out to Roxy, who took it.

"I knew you'd be back," the girl said, and tugged her toward the stairway.

***

Jeff Wheeler rolled over in bed and looked at the naked redhead next to him. She was pretty enough, with smooth skin, freckles on her large breasts, and fiery red hair between her legs, but she wasn't Roxy Doyle. Still, he had enjoyed her well enough.

She was lying on her back, breathing heavily, her generous breasts heaving.

"Is it over?" she asked, turning her head to look at him.

"It's far from over," Wheeler said, feeling out of breath, himself. He'd had sex with two beautiful redheads in two days, every man's dream, but it wasn't all that he wanted. "We're just startin'."

"How long do I have to hide?" she asked.

"Everybody thinks you're dead," he reminded her, "three times. You can't be seen."

"And what about you?"

"I'll be here with you, for a while," he said, "but eventually I'll step out into the open."

"This girl must've really done something terrible to you for you to plan all this."

"She did," he said. "Three-and-a-half years ago."

"And you waited this long for your revenge?"

"I had to strike it rich before I could get revenge," he said, "and that's what I did."

"Silver, right?"

He nodded. "It took me three years, but I finally found a giant vein of silver."

"And you weren't satisfied just to be rich?"

"No," he said. "That was the real beginnin'."

"Well," she said, sliding her hand down over his belly to take hold of his cock again, "I'm with you."

He started to harden in her hand. "I can see that," he said, and rolled over toward her . . .

***

"How many rooms are up here?" Roxy asked.

"A dozen," Mandy said. She stopped at one door. "This one's mine. Should we go in?"

"That's not what I'm here for, Mandy."

The girl pouted. "Pity."

"Can we check the other rooms?"

"Sure," Mandy said, "but I gotta warn you, most of them are in use."

"What about the girls downstairs?"

"Some of them share a room," she said, "but you should remember that I have my own. No sharin'."

"I'll remember," Roxy promised.

"This is Jenny's room." Mandy knocked and opened the door.

A naked woman with what seemed like miles of black hair and pale flesh turned to look at them. She had large, pendulous breasts with dark brown nipples. The man she was sitting astride also looked.

"Hey! What the—" he snapped.

"Sorry," Roxy said, "wrong man."

They closed the door and moved to the next one.

In this room a long, lean naked blonde with small tits was riding a man while facing the other way. He was concentrating on her butt when the door opened, so he craned his neck to look around her.

"Hey there," he said, "more company?"

"Sorry," Roxy said, "wrong room."

"Hey, hey, it's the right room, darlin'—" he started, but she cut him off by closing the door.

"That was Angie," Mandy said. "She likes to ride the other way."

When they opened the third door they found a man and a woman, fully dressed, sitting on a bed playing cards.

"We still got time, Mandy," the girl said.

"Sorry to interrupt, Susie," Mandy said, and closed the door.

"They were still dressed," Roxy said.

"Some men just come here for company, not sex," Mandy said. "Usually, the married ones."

"Married men look for company?" Roxy asked.

"They want somebody to talk to other than the wives," Mandy explained. "And they're willin' to pay for it."

"It doesn't matter to me," Roxy said. "I just need to find this one man."

"Only one man is good enough for you?" Mandy asked.

"This man has information I need."

"What's his name?"

"Wheeler," Roxy said, "Jeff Wheeler. Do men use their real names when they come here?"

"Oh, sure," Mandy said, "it's us whores who use phony names. Look, why don't you just wait in my room and I'll see if I can find out if he's here, or if he was ever here. It shouldn't take long."

"All right."

Mandy walked her back to the door of her room.

"I won't be long."

Chapter Twenty-Five

The bed in the room was made, and seemed to have clean sheets, which surprised Roxy. She sat on it, because there was no place else to sit. The mattress was surprisingly firm.

She stood and walked to the window, looked out at an open field. If not for her gun she could have been condemned to a place like this, making her living on her knees and on her back. If not for a natural ability, and the friendship of Clint Adams, the Gunsmith, she could have been a whore. It was honest work, but not for her. She could not have done this . . .

The door opened and Mandy came back in.

"Your man was here," she said.

"When?"

"Last night."

"Who was he with?"

"A girl named Annabelle."

"Is she here now?"

"Yes."

"I'd like to speak with her."

"You can," Mandy said, "but first." She shrugged her shoulders and was suddenly naked, her clothes gathered around her ankles.

"Mandy—" Roxy said.

"Give me five minutes," she said, stepping toward Roxy, away from the crumpled garment, "if after five minutes you still want to leave this room, I'll take you to Annabelle."

"Mandy—"

"Three, then," the girl said, "three minutes."

Naked, Mandy walked to Roxy took her hands and said, "Sit on the bed."

Roxy sat, surprised that her breath was coming quickly.

Mandy knelt before her, took her face in her hands, and kissed her on the mouth. Roxy didn't move. She was surprised though, at how sweet the kiss was, how much more gentle than a man's lips Mandy's were. The whore drew her head back, looked into Roxy's eyes, then took Roxy's hand and placed it on one naked breast. It was like a peach, round and firm, but not large. Mandy's nipples were light brown. The girl opened Roxy's hand, pressed the palm to her nipples, and then made circles. When she took her hand away, Roxy's stayed. She felt the nipple on her palm, then took it in her fingers and pinched.

"Women know how to please a woman," Mandy whispered. "Doesn't that make sense?"

"You've been with women?" Roxy asked.

"When they come here, looking for it," Mandy said, shrugging. "It's business."

"But you prefer men?"

"I prefer beauty," Mandy said, "and I've never seen beauty like yours, before."

The girl leaned forward and kissed Roxy again. This time she reacted, kissed the girl back. But when their mouths parted Roxy whispered, "Your three minutes are up."

Mandy smiled. "You can be a bitch, huh?"

"Can't we all?' Roxy asked.

Mandy stood, walked to her dress, picked it up and stepped back into it.

"Come on," she said. "I'll take you to Annabelle."

Roxy stood, her legs slightly weak, and followed the girl from the room.

Mandy took Roxy down the hall.

"Why didn't we look in here before?" she asked.

"Annabelle's not workin', today."

"Why not?"

"You'll see."

Mandy opened the door and they went in. There was a woman with red hair lying on a bed with her back to the door.

"Annabelle?" Mandy said.

The woman turned over to look at them. One eye was swollen shut, and both eyes were blackened.

"Jesus," Roxy said.

She walked to the bed to look closer at the woman. She was about her age, not built the same, but with the same red hair. She couldn't tell if the face resembled hers, because it was so swollen.

"He did this?" she asked. "The man who was with you last night?"

"Yes." The woman was lucky. She apparently still had all her teeth, though her lips were swollen.

"Did he say anything?" Roxy asked.

"He just kept callln' me by the same name over and over again while he was hittin' me."

"What name?" Roxy asked, though she already knew.

"He kept callin' me "Roxy.'"

Roxy put her hand on Annabelle's shoulder.

"I'm so sorry."

"Are you Roxy?"

"Yes, I am."

Annabelle put her hand over Roxy's.

"You better watch out for him," she said. "He's crazy."

"I'm going to find him and make him pay for this," Roxy said.

"What did you do to make him hate you so much?" Annabelle asked.

"I'm going to find that out, too," Roxy said.

Chapter Twenty-Six

Roxy followed Mandy back down to the first floor, where a grinning Madam Rosie greeted them.

"Took a while," she said. "Find out, or do, anything interestin'?"

"You've got a battered redhead up there," Roxy said.

"Yeah, Annabelle," Rosie said. "Her guy went a little crazy on her. She'll be fine."

"Has she been seen by a doctor?"

"Yeah, the doc was here."

"What about the sheriff?"

"We don't need the law here," Rosie said, growing serious. "We handle our own problems."

"And how did you handle that customer after he almost beat her to death?"

"I had Conrad throw him out."

"Who's Conrad?"

Rosie pointed. When Roxy looked she saw a big black man who looked like his muscles had muscles.

"That's Conrad."

Roxy walked over to the big man.

"Did he put up a fight?" she asked, Conrad.

"No, he didn't," the man said in a surprisingly high voice for someone his size. "I walked him out."

"Was he armed?"

"Yeah, he had a gun."

"He didn't try to use it?"

"No," Conrad said. "If he had, I woulda made him eat it."

"So he just left?"

"He paid," Conrad said.

"How much?"

"A lot," Rosie said, from behind her. "A helluva lot."

Roxy turned back to her.

"Okay, I get it now."

"I get it, too," Rosie said. "He went upstairs with Annabelle because she had red hair—like yours. Why doesn't he just beat you up?"

Roxy thought that was a good question.

"You know what?" Rosie said. "I changed my mind. I'm takin' back my offer of a job for you."

"I'm crushed," Roxy said. She looked at Mandy. "Thanks."

"Any time," Mandy said.

Roxy went out the door, which Rosie slammed behind her. Nobody, not Rosie, or Mandy, or Annabelle, the girl he beat up, had gotten the man's name, but from Annabelle's description, and the fact that he kept calling her "Roxy," she was sure it had been Jeff Wheeler.

And with any luck, he was still in town.

***

Roxy went to the sheriff's office. Taggert was seated behind his desk, where he seemed to always be.

"Do you ever make rounds?" she asked.

"I do my job."

"You didn't do it last night."

"What are you talkin' about?"

"A woman was beaten half to death at Madam Rosie's," Roxy said.

"Rosie handles her own security, her own problems," Taggert said.

"Yeah," she said, "I met Conrad."

"If they didn't send for me, there's nothin' I can do."

Roxy pressed her lips together, then said, "You're probably right."

"Why do you feel so bad for a beat up whore?" he asked.

"Because she had red hair."

"Ah," he said, "you think your friend Wheeler beat her up instead of you."

"I do."

"So did he kill, or have the other three killed by someone else?"

She hesitated.

"What is it?"

"Something just occurred to me."

"What?"

"The one that was killed here. Did you see the body?"

"No."

"What about the men who were supposed to have killed her?" she asked.

"I didn't get to talk to them," he said. "They lit out. But witnesses said—"

"Did the witnesses examine the body?"

"No, I don't think so. What's your point?"

"How do we know there's even a body in that grave?" she asked.

"You think the town buried an empty casket?"

"I don't know."

He laughed. "So what do you wanna do, dig 'er up?"

Roxy didn't answer.

"You wanna dig 'er up, don't you?"

"Yes."

"And if it's empty?"

"I'll go and check the other two?"

"And if they're empty?" he asked. "What will it mean?"

"Probably that this was a trap for me."

"And you walked right into it?"

"Yes."

"The mayor's not gonna go for that."

"So we don't tell him."

"Yeah, and there goes my job."

"So then you don't know about it, either."

"You gonna dig it up yourself?"

"If I have to," she said.

"No wait," Taggert said. "Xander."

"Xander Tyler?"

Taggert nodded. "He'll dig it up for you. You've met him?"

"Once, in the livery," she said. "Isn't he . . . kind of ancient?"

"Not as ancient as you'd think," Taggert said, "and he's strong as a bull."

"He's the one who told me about Telegraph."

"Why would he do that?"

"Because I paid him, and because he knew who I was."

"Xander can confirm that you're the real Lady Gunsmith?" Taggert asked.

"Yes."

"Why didn't you tell me that before?"

"I left town right after he told me, and then things started to happen. I haven't had a chance."

"Well, find him and give him a shovel," the lawman said. "He'll dig it up."

"Why would he do that?" she asked.

"Because," he said, "you'll pay him."

PART TWO

Chapter Twenty-Seven

Roxy went to the place she first—and last—saw Xander, the livery stable. She didn't know whether he worked there or not, but that was where he wanted to meet, so she took a chance.

It was late. The livery was closed, and dark, but the front doors were ajar. She went inside, found the same lantern that had been lit last time was lit again.

"Xander?"

No answer.

"Xander Tyler, you here? It's Roxy Doyle."

The man appeared from the darkness, the same tall and dark figure of indeterminate age.

"What are you doin' here?" he asked. "Did you go to Telegraph?"

"I did," she said, "and to Vinton."

"Yeah, I heard about that place, too. So whataya doin' back here?"

"This is where it started for me," she said. "And this is where I'm going to find out the truth."

"How you gonna do that?"

"First," she said, "by digging up a grave."

He smiled at that, revealing sharp but yellowed teeth.

"You gonna do that?" he asked. "Dig up yer own grave?"

"All three, if I have to," she said, "but I'll start with this one."

"And whataya hope to find?"

"I know what I think I'm going to find."

"What's that?"

"Nothing."

Xander cackled. "That'd fix this town good, if'n it was found out they buried them an empty casket."

"That's the point," she said, "but I need your help."

"How so?"

"I can't dig it up on my own."

"You look like a strong girl, to me."

"Well . . . I don't have a shovel."

"I got shovels."

"More than one?"

He frowned, maybe figuring if he answered that one he was trapped.

But in the end he said, "Yeah."

"Then you'll help me dig?"

"When?"

"Tonight," she said, "now."

"In the dark?" he asked.

"We'll use a lamp," she said, "and the moon."

"And if we get caught?"

"Then I'll be using more than just a shovel," she said, touching her gun.

He cackled again. "That's good enough for me. I'll get the shovels." But he turned, and then turned back right away. "You are payin' me, right?"

They walked in the dark to Boot Hill, each carrying a shovel. They could hear the revelry emanating from the saloons, possibly some folks still celebrating the burial of Lady Gunsmith. With any luck, within the hour, Roxy would prove them more than wrong. Not only was she not in this grave, but maybe nobody was.

"Okay," she said, when they reached the wooden marker, "let's do it fast."

She removed the marker, laid it aside, and they started digging.

They were halfway down when they noticed somebody walking up the slope towards them.

"We maybe got trouble," Xander announced.

But as the man came closer, Roxy saw his face in the moonlight and recognized Sheriff Taggert.

"I thought I'd find you two up here."

"You here to arrest us?" Roxy asked.

"Naw," he said, "just keep diggin'. I'm here to make sure there's no gunplay if you get caught."

By the time their shovels struck the top of the wooden casket no one else had come along.

"Okay," Roxy said to Xander, "time to light the lamp."

Xander picked up the oil lamp they had brought with them but had not yet lit for fear they'd attract attention. But now it was time to open the casket and have a look. He struck a match and lit the lamp. It cast an eerie yellow light over the scene.

Sheriff Taggert moved closer to the action, wanting to get a good look, himself.

Roxy dug the tip of the shovel beneath the casket's lid and pried it up, then moved along to the next nail and did the same. When she got the last nail taken care of, she put the shovel down, yanked the lid and slid it off.

"Damn," Taggert said.

She looked up at the two men, and Xander brought the lamp closer. But it didn't matter. Even in the moonlight they could see that the casket was filled with rocks to weigh it down. There was no body.

"Now what?" Taggert asked.

Chapter Twenty-Eight

Fran Dunston, naked on the bed, watched Jeff Wheeler get dressed.

"Do you have to go?" she asked.

"Yeah, I do," he said. "I still have some arrangements to make."

"What kind of arrangements?" she asked.

"That's not for you to know."

"This is still about her?"

"This will always be about her."

"Why don't you just kill her?" Fran asked.

"That would be too easy," Wheeler said. "I could hide on a roof, or in a hotel room at a window, and shoot her in the back with a rifle. Or break into her room and kill her."

"Like you did to me in one of my deaths," she said.

"That's right."

"Jeff." She got off the bed and walked to him. He took in her nude body again, breasts, hips, freckles, all very like Roxy Doyle, but somehow not.

She put her hands on his shoulders. "Why don't we just leave? You and me. Go somewhere together, forget all about this Lady Gunsmith."

"I can't."

"I'm not enough?" Fran asked. "After all I've done for you?"

"After all you've done for me, Franny," he said, "why would I let it all go to waste, now?"

Crestfallen, she took her hands off his shoulders, walked to the bed and sat.

"So I just wait here?"

"Right," he said. "Wait here, stay inside, don't let anyone see you. I'll bring you some food."

"I liked it better when I was in Sunset, and Telegraph, even Vinton," she said. "When people were afraid of me and givin' me anythin' I wanted."

"They weren't afraid of you, Fran," Wheeler said, "they were afraid of Lady Gunsmith."

"Yeah," she said, "I know. And you're not in love with me, you're in love with her."

"If I'm in love with her," he said, "why am I plannin' on killin' her?"

"That's a question you're gonna have to answer for yourself," she said.

He strapped on his gun, grabbed his hat and made for the door.

"What if you don't come back?" she asked.

"If I'm not back in the mornin'," he said, "you can leave, Fran. Go wherever you want."

"I'll give you til tomorrow night, Jeff," Fran said. "I'll be here."

He nodded, and left.

***

They decided not to rebury the casket. After all, why bother? There was no body. And leaving it open would allow anyone else who came along to see that.

Roxy decided that the next day she would ride to Telegraph, and then Vinton if she had time, and dig up both of those graves.

"They're going to be empty, too," she told Xander and Taggert.

"But why?" Xander asked. "What's the point?"

"To make the town famous," Taggert said.

"Not even that," Roxy said. "I think the point was to get me here."

"But didn't you ride in anyway," Taggert asked, "during the burial?"

"I hate to say it, but that was coincidence," Roxy admitted. "But if I had heard news of Lady Gunsmith being shot and buried in three different towns, I would have come, anyway."

Taggert looked at Xander. "And you're sure she's the real McCoy?"

"She's the real deal, Sheriff."

Taggert shook his head. "So there's no body, but there was a woman with red hair, wearing a gun, callin' herself Lady Gunsmith. What happened to her?"

"That's one of the things I'm going to find out," Roxy said.

"Are we done here?" Xander asked.

"We're done," Roxy told him. "Thanks for your help, Xander. You can take your shovels."

119

Xander picked up both shovels and looked at Roxy. "You wanna pay me to do anythin' else, let me know."

"I will," she said. "Thanks."

Xander walked off down the hill and into the shadows.

"You gonna ride to Telegraph alone?" Sheriff Taggert asked.

"Unless you want to come with me?"

"I wouldn't have any authority there."

"Then I'll go on my own," she said, "but I'll be back as soon as I prove those other two graves are empty."

"Somebody must have a real grudge against you to try to set this up," he said.

"That's why I'm looking for Wheeler," she said. "It might be him."

"Well," Taggert said, "if you can't find him, maybe now that you've dug this up, he'll find you."

"That would suit me," she said, "just fine."

Chapter Twenty-Nine

Roxy never did speak with the sheriff in Telegraph. As she rode into the small town again the next morning she wondered if she'd be able to get the casket dug up without running into the law. She remembered his name was Cotton Manning, and she'd been told he was an inept lawman. So maybe she could do this just fine without involving him.

But she knew of someone who might help her . . .

She made her way to the whorehouse, dismounted and approached the front door. She didn't know the girl who answered her knock, but she asked if she could see Mandy.

"Come on in, sweetie," the girl said. "She's in the parlor."

The girl led her to the room, where Mandy was sitting with a young man. However, as soon as she saw Roxy, she left him and walked over to her.

"You came back," she said. "I knew you would."

"I need to talk to you, Mandy."

"Talk?"

"Just talk."

Mandy shrugged. "We still gotta go upstairs. You still gotta pay."

Roxy's money was dwindling, but she thought she had enough for a conversation with a whore.

"Okay."

"Follow me."

Mandy rook Roxy's hand and led her up the stairs, to her room. Inside, the girl walked to the bed and sat down.

"Come," she said, "sit."

"I'll stand," Roxy said.

Mandy smiled a very pretty smile. "Are you afraid of me?"

"Not afraid," Roxy said, "I just want to keep our minds on business."

"Business?" Mandy asked. "I do have my mind on my business."

"Look, Mandy, I need help."

"To do what?"

"Dig up a grave."

"A grave?" Mandy asked, frowning. "Why would you wanna dig up a grave?"

"To prove that it's empty."

"Why would you wanna prove it's—oh, wait. I think I get it. Rosie told me you said you were Roxy Doyle."

"And she believes me."

"Yeah.

"Do you believe me?"

"Sure," Mandy said, with a shrug, "why not? So you wanna dig up your own grave and prove it's empty."

"Right."

"Prove it to who?"

"Everybody," Roxy said.

"So how do you expect me to help?"

"I need to dig up the grave," Roxy said. "I don't want to do it alone and I don't even have any shovels."

"I can probably get you a couple," Mandy said, "but I'm not about to do any diggin'."

"I didn't think you would," Roxy said. "But maybe you know somebody who would."

"As a favor?"

"That would be nice."

Mandy studied her for a moment.

"You'd probably have to pay," she said, then.

"I don't have much money."

"I don't suppose I could use this to get you into bed with me."

"Mandy," Roxy said, "like I've said before, you're very pretty, and you smell really nice, but . . ."

"Okay," Mandy said, "I have an idea about somebody, but you'll have to work it out with him."

"How?"

"That's up to you." She got up off the bed. "I'll bring him in."

"He's in the house?" Roxy asked.

"He works for us."

Mandy went out the door before Roxy could ask more questions. She went and sat down on the bed, wondering what she was getting herself into?

Ten minutes later the door opened and Mandy walked in, followed by the big black man, Conrad.

"Roxy, you've met Conrad."

"I have," Roxy said. "Will he take me to the man who's going to help me?"

"No," Mandy said, "he is the man who's going to help you."

Conrad stared at her, silently.

"What's the price?" Roxy asked.

"That's up to you and him," Mandy said. She backed out of the room, closing the door behind her.

"Okay, Conrad," she said, "did Mandy tell you what I need?"

"She did." The high voice jarred her, again.

"I don't have much money—"

"I don't want your money."

"Then what do you want?"

Conrad unbuttoned his shirt and took it off, revealing a chest that looked as if it had been chiseled from stone. Then he unbuttoned his trousers and dropped them to the floor. A huge erection jutted out from his crotch, easily the largest she'd ever seen. It was smooth, and ebony, and made her breath come faster.

"Oh," she said.

Chapter Thirty

"So this is what you want?" she asked.

"From the first minute I saw you."

"And then you'll help me?"

"Yes."

It was a big trade off, but she couldn't keep her eyes off his body, and even if there was no trade to make, her legs felt weak and her heart was racing. She wanted him, and she didn't like it. With most of her sexual encounters—like with the bartender, Wheeler—she was the one in charge. She couldn't afford to have that change.

"All right," she said, then, as he stepped forward she blurted, "but on my terms."

He stopped.

"Just . . . wait," she said, and started to undress.

There was an ornate metal bedpost, on which she hung her gunbelt. Then she sat on the bed, removed her boots and tossed them away. Standing, she unbuttoned her trousers and let them drop, stepped out of them. Her shirt was next, the camisole and underwear. When she stood up straight she was as naked as he was, and his breathing was coming as fast as hers. And if anything, his erection had gotten larger.

"You're a beautiful woman," he said, breathlessly.

"And you're a beautiful looking man," she said. "But you know that."

"Then we're a lot alike," he said, folding his arms across his massive chest. "Neither of us has any doubts."

"You sound educated," she said. "You were never a slave, were you?"

"No," he said, "I came to this country a free man, and I stayed that way. Came West a while back from New York."

"Why would you do that?"

"It's a long story," he said, "and we don't have time for that now, do we?"

"No," she said, "we don't. But we have time for this."

She stepped forward, closing the distance between them. He dropped his arms to his side and she ran her palms over his chiseled chest. It was hairless, and smooth. She could feel the heat coming off his body. Gliding her hands down over his belly she took his cock in her hands, stroked it. A moan sounded from deep inside him, but he kept his lips tight. She continued to slide one hand up and down him, reaching with the other to cradle his sack.

Holding him that way she began to back toward the bed, tugging him along. He went willingly, otherwise she never would have been able to move him.

When the back of her legs hit the bed she turned him, and sat him down. She knelt between his spread knees. She had never been with a black man before. She ran her hands up his chest again, around his neck, and then kissed him, liking the feel of his lips on hers. Just as he started to lean into the kiss, though, she pulled away.

"Uh-uh," she said. "Not yet."

He brought his hands up, started to reach for her breasts. She slapped them away.

"Not yet for that, either."

"You're in charge," he said, putting his hands down flat on the mattress, on either side. "Is that what you want to hear?"

"Yes," she said, rubbing her palms over his muscular thighs, "that's what I want to hear."

He had possibly the most perfect body she had ever seen, and she wished she had the time to explore it more thoroughly. But she knew what he wanted, and what she needed, so she turned her attention back to his huge cock. Taking it in both hands she leaned over him and licked the bulging head. As she got it wet it seemed to gleam. The effect on her was almost hypnotic. She wanted the whole thing to gleam like that, so she began to lick the length of it, wetting it, making him moan. She looked up at him, locked eyes, smiled, and then opened her mouth to take him inside. At first she thought he was going to be too thick for her, but she managed to get her lips around the head, and the rest just slid in. She enjoyed how hot and smooth the skin was, and he obviously enjoyed what she was doing. She sucked him that way for a few minutes, feeling the muscles in his thighs tense beneath her palms. He groaned again, very loudly, and she knew it was time.

She released him from her mouth and pushed him down onto his back.

"Slide up," she said. "Get all the way on to the bed."

He did as she asked, so that his legs were not dangling. She scooted up onto him, sat on him, trapping his penis between them. Leaning over, she kissed him again, this time fully, mouth opened, tongue working, while she slid her wet pussy up and down on him, wetting him again but with different juices, this time.

Finally, she broke the kiss, sat up straight, raised her hips and brought herself down on him. That huge, swollen head of his cock popped through the lips of her vagina, and then she sat down on him. His eyes went wide as she took as much of him as she could inside, her own breath catching in her throat. Jesus, but he filled her up!

"We're going for a ride now, Conrad," she whispered to him. gliding up and down on his cock, "let's see which one of us gets to the end of the trail first."

Chapter Thirty-One

Roxy offered to help Conrad dig, but he told her to just step aside, and then he went to work with the shovel. This time she hadn't waited to do it in the dead of night. It was broad daylight, and she fully expected to meet Sheriff Cotton Manning any minute now. Enough people had seen what they were doing, and she knew somebody would go to the law.

Sure enough, a tall, grey-haired man with a badge on his chest came up the hill toward them just as Conrad's shovel struck the lid of the coffin.

"Conrad," he said, obviously recognizing the black man, "you mind tellin' me what the hell you think you're doin'?"

Conrad stood up straight. He had removed his shirt and his torso was slick with sweat, the flesh as shiny as his penis had been when Roxy climbed off him about an hour earlier.

"Ask the lady, Sheriff," Conrad said. "I'm just doing what I'm paid to do."

Manning shook his head, looked at Roxy.

"He's one educated nigger, ain't he?" he asked. "Talks real pretty."

"I'm Roxy Doyle, Sheriff Manning." Roxy said. "This is supposed to be my grave, but it's not."

"And you expect me to just believe that?" the lawman asked. "That you're not just a coupla grave robbers after the body of a famous gunfighter? What are you gonna do, put it on display in some museum?"

"I'm Roxy Doyle, Sheriff," she said, "and I ain't in some grave."

Manning looked at the hole Conrad had dug, then back at Roxy.

"Okay, prove it."

"Conrad," Roxy said.

The big black man nodded, and used the shovel to pry the lid off the coffin. When it came up, he lifted it and tossed it aside.

Manning took two steps forward and peered into the grave. What he saw made his mouth fall open.

"Sonofabitch," he said.

"Sorry, Sheriff," Roxy said, "but your town ain't becoming famous, this year."

Manning stared at her.

"So," he said, "you're Lady Gunsmith."

"That's right," she said. "I am. And I'd like to know if you have any idea who's responsible for this little charade."

"Burying an empty coffin?" Manning asked. "I don't have any idea, Miss Lady Gunsmith. All I know is some red-haired woman came to town, claimed to be you, and was apparently shot for her trouble."

"By who?"

"I can't tell you that," Manning said, "any more than I can tell you what happened to her, if she's not in that coffin—which, obviously, she isn't."

"So what do you plan to do about this?" she asked.

"I'll ask some questions, and see what I can find out," he said, "but frankly, I don't see that any law's been broken. I mean, somebody buried an empty coffin." He shrugged. "What would I charge them with? And if I found whoever supposedly shot Lady Gunsmith, well . . . they didn't, did they?"

"So you're not going to do anything?"

"I think the question is, what are you gonna do?" Manning asked.

"Well," she said, "right now I'm going to buy Conrad a beer. He deserves it."

"And what about this hole?" Manning asked.

"You can use it for the next legitimate funeral you have in town," she said. "Conrad?"

The big black man climbed out of the hole, grabbed his shirt and followed Roxy down the hill.

Chapter Thirty-Two

Roxy took Conrad to the nearest saloon. As they entered he was buttoning his shirt. They were an odd pair, the beautiful redhead and the giant black man, and they drew looks as they approached the bar. The bartender watched, waiting for them to reach him.

"Two beers, bartender," Roxy said.

"Comin' up," the man said.

When Roxy and Conrad had their beers they leaned on the bar and drank. Others in the place gave them a lot of room, not that there were many of them.

"What do you intend to do now?" Conrad asked.

"I'm not sure."

"Do you want to go to Vinton and dig up the third grave?" he asked. "I can ride there with you."

"I don't really think that's going to be necessary, Conrad," she said. "It's pretty clear now that the Vinton grave will also be empty."

"So then, back to Sunset?" he asked.

"Yeah," she said, "back to Sunset, I guess. I think that's where it's all going to end."

"Do you want me to go with you?" he asked again.

"No," she said, "you did your part." She smiled at him. "You've done more than your part, haven't you?"

"I don't know," he said. "You're in charge. You tell me."

"Yes," she said, touching his arm, "you did more than your part, all right."

"I like you," he said. "You're not like those women at the house."

"What do you mean?"

"They allow themselves to be used by men, for money," he said. "With you, it's the other way around."

"Most men would say that makes me a bossy bitch."

"It makes you a strong woman," he said. "Take my advice and stay that way. It will serve you well throughout your life."

"You sound like a wise old man," she said.

"How old are you?" he asked.

"I'm twenty-five," she answered.

He smiled at her. "I'm fifty-one. Twice your age."

Her mouth fell open. What was it about black men that made it so difficult to guess their age? If he looked this way at 51, what had he looked like as a younger man?

"I'm shocked," she said.

"You have a long life ahead of you," he said. "With any luck you'll be shocked a lot, before you become old and cynical, like me."

"What are you doing here?" she asked. "I mean, in this town and that job? You're an educated man."

"This is the West," he said. "There's not much use for an educated black man out here."

"And in the East?"

"It was pretty much true there, as well," he said. "So I'm just living my life as best I can."

"What do you do when you're by yourself, in your room" she asked.

"I read," he said. "I like Mark Twain, Dickens, Edgar Allan Poe, Robert Louis Stevenson. I've read as much as I can get my hands on about King Arthur and the Knights of the Round Table."

Roxy was surprised, again. The only other man she'd ever met who read all of that was Clint Adams.

"I've read Twain," she admitted, "but other than that, just some dime novels."

"I'll bet they used to be interesting," he said to her, "but now they're about you."

"Well," she said, "not yet."

"Give it time," he said. "They will be."

They finished their beers and then stepped outside.

"I need a bath," he said. "I smell like a mule."

"You smell fine" she said. "Like a man."

"Care to join me in a hot tub?" he asked.

"I'd love to," she said, "but if I do, I won't get back to Sunset for days."

"Then come back and see me," he said, "when it's all over, before you leave the area."

"I'll do that, Conrad," she said. "I promise."

Chapter Thirty-Three

Jeff Wheeler walked into the small saloon in Sunset, The Wild Jack. Two men were waiting for him at a back table, with a bottle of whiskey. He stopped at the bar for a third glass before joining them.

As he sat, one of them filled his empty glass.

"We was wonderin' when you'd show up," the other one said. His name was Nick Owens, the other man was Carlos Montalvo.

"I had to make sure the bitch was out of town," Wheeler said. "I don't want her seein' us together."

"Are you ready to take her?" Owens asked.

"Almost," Wheeler said. "She just dug up the grave and saw that it was empty. I figure she's ridin' to Telegraph and Vinton to find out if those graves are empty, too."

"And then?" Owens asked. Montalvo was a quiet one. He drank, and listened.

"It'll play in her head," Wheeler said. "The who, and the why. And then she'll start wonderin' . . . when?"

"Does she know it's you who's after her?" Owens asked.

"I don't know," Wheeler said. "She should, by now. It depends on whether or not she remembers my brother's name."

"Well, when are you gonna find out?" Owens asked.

"Whata you care?" Wheeler asked. "You're gettin' paid, aren't you?"

"We better be gettin' paid," Owens said. "We ain't seen any money, yet."

"If you two and me kill Lady Gunsmith," Wheeler said, "you'll be able to name your own price, anyplace you go."

"Yeah, well, right now we just want what you promised us," Owens said, and at that Montalvo nodded.

"Don't worry," Wheeler said. "You'll get your money. For now, why don't we just get some more whiskey?"

Wheeler stood up and went to the bar to get the bottle. When he'd first concocted this scheme to get revenge on Roxy Doyle all he wanted was to lure her to New Mexico and kill her. But after that night when she invited him to her room, he started to think differently about killing her.

Later still, though, after the way she rushed him out of her room when she was done with him, his mind went back to his original plan. Lure her to New Mexico, make sure she remembered what had happened in Buffalo, Wyoming, in front of the Occidental, and then kill her, making sure she knew why she was dying, and who was killing her. It was silly to think one night in bed with her might have changed his attitude.

He took the bottle from the bartender and went back to the table with his two hired guns.

Chapter Thirty-Four

Roxy rode back to Sunset, once again secured a spot for her horse at the livery, and for herself at a hotel. Both of those chores done, she made her way to a small café for a meal. Instead of her usual beef stew—how could anybody ever ruin that—she decided this time on a steak supper with all the trimmings. She wanted a long, leisurely meal so she could ponder her options and decide how to proceed.

First, she wondered just how much she should include Sheriff Taggert in her plans? Not that he was a terribly impressive starpacker, but he was the local law and, if push came to shove, she would end up dealing with him sooner or later.

When the waitress brought her meal she set it down with a big smile and said, "Honey, I could tell just lookin' at you that you're a gal with a good appetite. So I made sure there was plenty of extra vegetables on the plate, and I went back to the kitchen to find you the biggest steak there."

Roxy knew the woman was not insinuating that she was fat. She knew she was a big, solid girl, and the woman was right, she did have a big appetite.

"Thank you," she said, and dug in.

The steak and vegetables went down easy, chased by a cold mug of beer. Afterwards, pie and coffee completed the meal, and Roxy knew what she was going to do.

She was going to wait . . .

Jeff Wheeler left his two gunmen with half of the second bottle of whiskey to consume. He didn't warn them about getting drunk. They were grown men who knew their own limits. If they got too drunk to shoot straight, they'd be paying the price.

But Wheeler, himself, he still had some more mind games to play with Roxy Doyle before he actually killed her. And that meant going out on the street, and letting her find him.

Wheeler's pride was still stinging from the way she'd treated him that night, after they had sex. But that sting was still nothing compared to having her kill his brother. And for what? Back then it wasn't even Gavin Doyle they were all waiting for in Buffalo. It turned out to be a phony version of the bounty hunter.

So his brother was killed for no reason.

He was going to make sure she knew that.

***

Roxy sat in a chair in front of her hotel and watched the people of Sunset go by. Sitting there that way reminded her again of the events that took place in Buffalo, Wyoming. How odd it was to connect Jeff Wheeler to those incidents, at a time when someone was impersonating her father. And now, here she was dealing with a situation where somebody was impersonating her.

It was through Wheeler that she was going to find the woman, and prove that the ex-bartender had put her up to it, just to lure Roxy to Sunset, Telegraph and/or Vinton. The only part of all this she couldn't understand was that she had ridden into Sunset, completely of her own accord, just at the time they were burying the coffin of the third phony lady Gunsmith.

What could that possibly be called, other than a coincidence? And for a woman who didn't believe in that word, how was she supposed to make sense of it all?

She was feeling remarkably relaxed as her mind swirled with questions. And then she thought about the time she had spent with Conrad in bed, and her body started to tingle. The man was an amazing specimen, no matter what his age, and she couldn't remember enjoying a man's body as much as she had enjoyed his. It made her time with Wheeler seem silly by comparison. That had just been a need that night, and it could have been any penis. On the other hand, Conrad was a special specimen.

She was still thinking about Conrad when she saw a man walking across the street, and recognized him. But she kept her seat, determined to make Jeff Wheeler come to her.

Chapter Thirty-Five

Wheeler was surprised to see Roxy sitting right out in front of the hotel, slouched in a chair as if she didn't have a care in the world. Wasn't she supposed to be out looking for him? He knew she'd been asking about him for a while, but what was going on now?

He decided the best thing to do was just confront her, and seem as relaxed as she seemed.

He crossed the street . . .

As Wheeler stepped into the street and started across, Roxy had the urge to draw her gun and shoot him. It was against all the advice and training she'd gotten from the Gunsmith to do such a thing, so she simply watched as he approached. Unlike the other times she had seen him, he was wearing a gun.

Instead of coming directly at her, he veered off, found a chair in front of another storefront, brought it over and sat on her right. She didn't like the location, so she subtly angled her chair that way, in case she needed to get her gun out and point it his way.

"I hear you been lookin' for me?" he asked. "Guess you shouldn't have kicked me out of your room so fast that night, huh?"

"Don't flatter yourself," she said. "My looking for you has nothing to do with that and everything to do with Buffalo, Wyoming."

"Ah," he said, "you remember now."

"I don't remember you," she said, "but I do remember killing . . . who? Your brother? Cousin?"

"My brother." He realized he was gritting his teeth, so he took a moment to relax, again.

"What was his name?"

"Andrew."

"Well," she said, "Andrew must have fallen in with a couple of bad pennies."

"He made his own friends," Wheeler said. "But we stayed close. He was there to see me."

"He was there to kill a man he thought was my father, Gavin Doyle."

"The bounty hunter?"

"That's right."

"I heard the fella claiming to be Doyle was a fake."

"He was," she said. "I chased him out of town, and then left, myself."

"Pausing to kill my brother and his friends."

"That happened before I knew a man was masquerading as my father. They thought the same thing."

"You didn't have to kill them."

"You're right," she said. "I didn't. I gave them the choice to walk away, and they didn't take it."

"I'm not lookin' for the reason you killed them," Wheeler said, "I just know that you did."

"And how do you know that?"

"I told you, I saw you do it, in the Occidental. I was there."

She studied his face.

"I don't remember you."

"I was nobody," he said.

"And since then?"

"I hit it big," he said, "went into prospectin' and found silver."

"Congratulations," she said. "Why come after me after three-and-a-half years later?"

"Because I have the money to come after you, now," he said. "And the skills."

"You think so?"

"I know so," he said. "Remember, I saw you kill them. I know your move. And I'm better."

"And if you've gotten better over the years," she said, "don't you think I may have?"

That seemed to stop him for a moment. Could it be possible he'd never thought of that?

"So, are you gonna offer me the chance to ride out of town?" he said, recovering his composure.

"No," she said.

"Why not?" he asked. "You claim that's what you did for my brother and his partners."

"This isn't the same. You're actually planning on killing me. And I want to know who the woman was who's been impersonating me," Roxy said. "I want to make sure she doesn't do it again."

"She's just somebody I hired," he said. "You won't have to worry about her anymore."

"I'll make that judgment."

"You'll have to live through this to do that," he reminded her.

"Tell me," she said, ignoring that comment, "why three graves?"

"I thought one grave you could ignore, two might bring you lookin', but I was sure you wouldn't be able to resist three."

"I didn't come looking," she said. "I just happened to ride into Sunset during the burial."

"That don't matter," he said. "You woulda heard about it sooner or later. These towns really liked the idea. Word would have spread like wildfire."

"Well, it didn't," she said, "and it won't. I've proven those graves were empty. I don't think these folks are going to want you around much longer."

"Or maybe," he said, "they won't mind if the real Lady Gunsmith is killed in their town."

"Tell me where the girl is," Roxy said. "And what her name is?"

"Not gonna happen."

"I'll find her."

"I don't think so."

"I found you, didn't I?" she asked.

He stared at her. "Noooo, I found you."

"You just stopped hiding," she said.

"I'm not hidin'," he said. "Never was."

She turned, stared straight ahead, but was still able to watch him peripherally.

"You've got help, don't you?" she asked. "The men who are supposed to have killed me, three times. They're still here with you."

"I do have help," he said, standing, "and maybe the fourth time will be the charm."

"Don't count on it," she advised him.

Chapter Thirty-Six

Roxy was ready for Wheeler to try something right there and then, but instead he turned and walked away. She let him. He had no reason to hide, anymore. He'd make his move when he was ready. Meanwhile, she still had to find the woman. She was probably in a hotel room, so that's where she figured on starting.

She spent the afternoon checking hotels and rooming houses, asking about a red-haired woman.

"You mean like you?" one desk clerk asked.

"I mean exactly like me."

That clerk shook his head and said, "Oh, no, Ma'am, I woulda noticed if a woman who looks like you checked in here. Believe me."

She did. In each case she believed the clerk, or the person running the rooming house, that they had not seen or given a room to a woman who looked like Roxy.

Now she wondered, did the woman look like her when she first got to town, and did she still look that way now?

Roxy was ready to give up for the day, as it got dark. At least she'd managed to find Wheeler—or he found her—and they had both played their parts.

She wanted a beer but didn't want to stop into any saloon where she'd already been. Tucking her hair under her hat, she found a small place on a side street and stepped through the batwing doors.

"Beer," she told the bartender.

"This ain't no place for a lady," the rough looking, somewhat ugly man said. He had a scar across his cheek that was livid, and it reached to the corner of his mouth, permanently lifting that corner.

"You got beer?" she asked.

"Yeah, but—"

"Is it cold?"

"Well, yeah, of course."

"Then it's a place for this lady," she said. "Beer . . . please."

"Comin' up," the man said, with a shrug.

He drew her the beer and set it in front of her, then went to the far end of the bar, where three men were gathered. They immediately fell into a pitched conversation.

Roxy had chosen the place because she thought she might be able to have a drink and go unnoticed, but she should have known better. The town was all about the murder of a red-haired woman, and by now the word had probably gotten around about the empty grave. And the way the conversation was going at the end of the bar, she might not have as much time as she hoped to work things out with Wheeler.

She finished her beer and was about to leave when the three men came toward her, and the bartender returned. The other men in the place froze and watched.

"I warned you," he said to her, "this wasn't a good place."

"I guess you were right," she said.

The three men positioned themselves between her and the front door. They all wore guns, and looked like the kind of men who would use them.

"What's this about?" she asked them.

"Red hair," one of them said. "You've got it. Let's see it."

She hesitated, then removed her hat long enough for her hair to cascade down, then returned it to her head.

"Happy?"

"This town was gonna grow," one of them said. "We was gonna be famous, and you changed everything."

"How did I do that?"

"You dug up that empty grave," another said.

"So it's my fault the grave was empty?" she asked.

"It's your fault people know it's empty," the first man said.

"Bartender," she said, "who are these men?"

"Well, they're part of the town—"

"Names, please."

The bartender pointed at them in the order they had spoken. "That's Dack Evans—"

"First names will do," she said, cutting him off.

"Dack," the bartender said, pointing, "Bob and Freddie."

"Whataya care what our names are?" Dack asked.

"Well," she said, "Dack, Bob and Freddie, "it's because I hate to kill men whose names I don't know."

"Ha!" Bob said. "Yer gonna kill us?"

"Seems to me," she said, "that's where we're headed."

"That grave may be empty, but it's still dug," Dack said. "We need a dead red-haired girl to put in it."

"Yeah, see?" she said. "That's where we're headed all right."

Suddenly, she drew her gun and pointed it at the bartender's head.

"If that hand comes out from under the bar anything but empty, you're the first to die."

Slowly, he brought his hand up, empty.

"Now back away."

He did.

"And the three of you?" she asked. "Are you going to move out of my way?"

"We told you," Freddie said, "we need a dead red haired girl. Whether you're really Lady Gunsmith, or not."

Apparently, they didn't think she was.

"Then go ahead," she said. "Try it."

The three men hesitated, then Dack said, "Well, holster your gun so it's a fair fight."

"You're kidding, right?"

The three men looked confused.

"We can't exactly draw on you while you got your gun in your hand," Bob said.

"It ain't fair!" Freddie said.

"Who cares what's fair?" she asked. "I only care about walking out of here alive."

"This bitch is crazy," Dack said. "Let's get out of here." He looked at Roxy. "Another time."

The three men backed up, and then went out the batwing doors.

Roxy turned to look at the bartender, gun still in hand.

"And now you . . ."

Chapter Thirty-Seven

Sheriff Jack Taggert looked up as the door to his office opened and Jeff Wheeler entered.

"What the hell are you doin' here?" he demanded. "I told you not to come back."

"And I told you I'd be back when I needed your help," Wheeler reminded him.

Taggert pointed a finger at Wheeler.

"When you came up with this crazy scheme to bring Lady Gunsmith here, I told you I wouldn't help."

"Well," Wheeler said, "now she's here, and now you're gonna help."

"And why would I do that?" Taggert asked. "You can't force me to help."

"Maybe I can't force you," Wheeler said, "but I can pay you."

"You can't—"

"Ten thousand dollars."

Taggert stopped, thought a moment, then asked, "You have ten thousand dollars?"

"I do."

"And you'll give it to me?"

"To help me kill Lady Gunsmith," Wheeler said. "You won't have to work in this job anymore, and you can leave this town."

Taggert sat back in his chair. Ten thousand dollars was more money than he'd ever see in a lifetime.

"Jesus," he said, because he knew he was thinking about it.

"Jack," Wheeler said, "she trusts you, doesn't she?"

"I wouldn't say she trusts me," Taggert said. "But she talks to me."

"And she lets you get close," Wheeler said.

"Yeah," Taggert said, "but Jeff . . . I don't wanna be the one who kills her."

"No," Wheeler said, "I wanna do that. "I just want you to help me."

"So if I help you, I get the money?"

"That's right."

Taggert thought the proposition over.

"I'll need some of it up front," he decided. "As a show of good faith, on your part."

"And what do I get as a show of good faith?" Wheeler asked.

"Okay," Taggert said, "if we're gonna do this, we're just gonna have to trust each other . . . I guess."

"Well," Wheeler said, "we have known each other a long time."

"I left Buffalo, Wyoming long before you did, Jeff."

"Yeah," Wheeler said, "with my sister as your wife. But she never made it this far, did she?"

"That wasn't my fault, Jeff," Taggert said. "You know that. She got sick and . . . died."

"And you been buryin' yourself here ever since," Wheeler said. "Maybe it's time for you to start livin' again, and you can do that with ten thousand dollars."

"Yeah," Taggert said, "yeah, okay, Jeff. It's a deal."

Wheeler stepped forward. Taggert stood up, and the two shook hands.

"So, what do we do?" Taggert asked.

"We come up with a plan."

"I thought you had a plan," Taggert said.

"I did," Wheeler said, "a plan to bring her here. Now we need a plan to kill her."

"And you have more men?"

"I do."

"How many?"

"Two."

"And you think the four of us can kill her?"

"Like I said," Wheeler answered, "as long as we come up with a plan."

Chapter Thirty-Eight

The bartender stared down the barrel of Roxy's gun.

"What was all that about?" she asked.

"How would I know?" he demanded. "They're just a bunch of crazy cowboys."

"They didn't get the idea to confront me by themselves," she said. "You went to the end of the bar and told them to do it, or suggested they do it."

"Why would I do that?" he asked.

"I don't know," she said, "so I'll ask you again. Why would you do that?"

He stared at the little black hole at the end of her barrel, and then asked, "Could you point that somewhere else? It's makin' me real nervous."

"It's supposed to," she said, holding the gun steady. "Now give me an answer."

"Okay, look," he said, "you provin' that grave was empty? That pretty much killed this town, and if the town dies, so does my place."

"So you think that having me killed here will save you and the town."

"It wasn't my idea," the bartender insisted. "Somebody else thought it up, but it turned out to be a sham."

"And that justifies you trying to have me killed?" she asked.

He flapped his arms helplessly and said, "I'm sorry, I'm so sorry. I wasn't thinkin' straight."

"No, you weren't."

He closed his eyes.

"Please don't kill me," he said.

Roxy lowered her gun and holstered it.

"I'm not going to kill you—"

He opened his eyes, saw that the gun was gone, and breathed a sigh of relief.

"Thank you."

"—but if anybody comes after me and tells me you sent them, I'll be back."

"I won't," he said. "I swear. It was just . . . a mistake."

"It was a big mistake," she told him. "Remember that."

She walked to the batwings.

"Ma'am?" the bartender called out.

She turned as she got to the door. "Yes?"

"Are you really her?" he asked. "Lady Gunsmith, I mean."

"You better hope," she said, "that you never have to find out."

Chapter Thirty-Nine

Roxy left the saloon, her hands shaking because she had wanted to shoot someone. That wasn't a feeling she normally had. Clint Adams had taught her never to draw her gun unless she was going to use it. What she had done in the saloon was out of character for her, but maybe it was an indication of how this business of the three graves was really affecting her.

Perhaps what she should do was just find Jeff Wheeler again and call him out. He was obviously behind the three graves, so there was no mystery about it, anymore. Why not just get all this over with?

She was about to step into the street to cross when she saw Sheriff Taggert coming toward her.

"Sheriff," she said. "Are you looking for me?"

"I am," Taggert said, stopping as he reached her.

With him still in the street, and her on the boardwalk, she had to look down at him.

"What can I do for you?"

"You can give me your gun."

"What?"

"Yeah," Taggert said, "I think it's the only way to keep you from gettin' killed, or killin' somebody else."

"You're crazy."

"What?"

"If I walk around without a gun, that's a sure way to get killed, especially with Wheeler still in town."

"You're refusin' to give up your gun?"

"Damn right I'm refusing."

"I'm the law here, Miss Doyle."

"Yes, you are," she said, "but I'm still not givin' you my gun, so you're going to have to take it."

He stared up at her. She kept her hands at her sides, waiting for him to make a move. He may have been the law, but she wasn't about to let him disarm her. It would just be suicide. How could he not know that?

Or maybe he did.

***

Taggert was surprised to see Roxy enter his office. He had just gotten there a minute or so ago, himself.

"You change your mind?" he asked. "Come to turn in your gun?"

"No," she said, "I came to find out what your connection to Jeff Wheeler is."

"What are you talkin' about?" he asked.

"The only reason I can see for you to want to disarm me is to give Jeff Wheeler a clear chance at killing me. Why would you want to do that?"

"You're talkin' crazy."

"Am I?" Roxy asked. "If you don't tell me how you're involved, I'll have to find out for myself."

"Go ahead and try," Taggert said.

"Try?" Roxy said. "So that means there is a connection."

Taggert walked around his desk and dropped down heavily into his chair.

"Look," he said, "I was just tryin' to keep anybody from gettin' killed—"

"I don't believe that, Sheriff," Roxy said. "Not for one minute. I think you were trying to get me killed, which means I can't depend on you for anything—especially not for doing your job."

"Hey, wait a minute—"

She stormed to the door. "Stay clear of me, Sheriff. Out of my way. Understand?"

"You can't talk to me like—"

"Remember," she said, cutting him off and opening the door, "out of my way."

She walked out and slammed the door behind her.

Chapter Forty

Roxy knew she was alone now. Nobody to back her play. And she knew Wheeler wouldn't come after her alone. He'd have men with him, and he might even have Sheriff Taggert backing him.

All the more reason for her to find him and call him out. But not tonight. Not in the dark. She'd find him when the sun was high and force him to meet her on the street. And when he was dead and gone she'd put these three horrible towns behind her, towns that thought they could use her death to improve their lots.

She decided she'd had enough of saloons for one day, and returned to her hotel. She'd hold up in her room and get a good night's sleep. After a hearty breakfast in the morning she'd locate Jeff Wheeler and put an end to this entire charade that he had concocted.

And if Taggert got in the way, badge or not, she'd put him down, as well. She knew if she shot a lawman she'd be wanted, at least in New Mexico. She'd never been wanted for anything before, never walked on the wrong side of the law, but maybe it was time for a new experience.

***

Jeff Wheeler was staying in a small, deserted house he found on the edge of town. He was surprised when someone knocked on the door. He opened it and stared at Sheriff Jack Taggert.

"I thought we were gonna talk tomorrow," he said.

"I needed to see you now."

"Come on in."

Taggert entered, was brought up short when he saw the woman sitting on the bed. For just a moment he thought it was Roxy Doyle, but then he realized it was Wheeler's phony Lady Gunsmith. She was dressed, although her red hair looked disheveled. A gunbelt was hanging on a chair near her.

"That her?" Taggert asked. "She looks a little like her."

"She looks a lot like her, but that's not why you're here," Wheeler said. "Did you get it?"

"I went to her and told her I needed her gun," Taggert said.

"And?"

"She told me I'd have to take it from her."

"And you didn't do it," Wheeler said. "You weren't man enough."

"No, Jeff, I wasn't," the sheriff admitted. "Are you?"

"He's more than man enough," the redhead said.

"Shut up, Fran!" Wheeler snapped.

She fell silent, hurt.

"I shoulda known I couldn't count on you," Wheeler said to Taggert. "My sister couldn't, so why would I be able to."

That stung Taggert. There had been nothing he could do to save his wife once she got sick, and Wheeler knew that.

"You let Linda die," Wheeler went on, "and you're gonna let me die, too, right?"

"I'll be with you, Jeff," Taggert said. "If you die, I'm gonna die, too . . . like I shoulda died with Linda."

Suddenly, Wheeler relented. He reached out and put his hand on Taggert's shoulder.

"I'm sorry, Jack," he said. "I shoudn't've said any of that."

"No," Taggert said, "you shouldn't have, but you did." He backed away so that his brother-in-law's hand dropped from his shoulder. "I'll be around, Jeff. You just tell me when."

"I will, Jack."

Taggert looked at the woman again, then turned and went out the door.

"You didn't have to do that," Fran said.

"I know," Wheeler said, turning to her. "I just wanted to get him riled up."

"No," she said, "I meant you didn't have to tell me to shut up in front of him."

He walked to where she was sitting and took her face in his hands.

"Okay, I'm sorry," he said. "Instead of gettin' him riled, thinkin' about my sister, it got me riled."

She put her arms around his waist and pressed her cheek to him, hugging him tightly.

"I forgive you," she said, "but you have to let me help you."

"Whatayou mean?"

She drew her head back and looked up at him.

"Let me stand with you," she said. "I'll back your play. That gunbelt isn't just for show. One of the reasons you picked me for this job was that I can use it."

"You're not as good as she is," he warned her.

"Maybe not," she said, "but I can help you."

He stepped back watched as she stood up and reached for her gunbelt, then strapped it on.

"I'm ready, Jeff," she said.

"I can see that," Wheeler said. "Okay, then, you'll be part of this. You'll be in at the end."

She drew her gun, a quick move, and then slid it back in her holster.

"I'm ready."

Chapter Forty-One

Roxy woke the next morning, determined to finish her business in Sunset on that day. All she had to do was find Jeff Wheeler, and kill him.

Simple, right?

Not if the sheriff of Sunset intended to stand with him.

Over breakfast she started to think that the smartest course of action would be to keep Wheeler and Taggert separate. And she thought she knew how to do it, possibly without firing a shot.

"More coffee?" the young waiter asked. He looked very hopeful that she would accept, and therefore stay seated a little longer. He was smitten with her as soon as she walked through the door.

"No, thanks," she said. "I've had enough."

"Really?" he asked. "I could bring you more bacon. More biscuits?"

"I'll just pay my bill," she told him.

He looked crestfallen.

She paid for her breakfast and left the heartbroken waiter in her wake, like many other men.

***

Roxy went to the sheriff's office, but Taggert wasn't behind his desk. He might have actually been out doing his job, for a change. Or he might have been with Jeff Wheeler.

She walked across the street, where there were several small shops. One of them was closed, so she backed into the doorway and waited.

After about an hour, Sheriff Taggert appeared, walking down the street, alone, at a brisk pace. She waited until he went inside the office, waited a bit longer, then crossed over and opened the door.

As Taggert turned from whatever he was doing to see who it was, she drew her gun and pointed it at him. It occurred to her that she had already done that too many times. Clint Adams would have her head if he knew.

"What the—" Taggert said.

Turned out he was in the act of hanging his gunbelt on a wall peg.

"Finish what you were doing, Sheriff."

"What are you—"

"Hang the gun up!"

Taggert obeyed.

"Now step away from it, please."

Taggert took a few steps back.

"Good. Now, into the cell block."

"What are you gonna do?" Taggert asked.

"I'm taking you out of the pot, Sheriff," she told him. "The game's over for you."

"Are you gonna kill me?" Taggert asked. "Is that it?" His eyes went to his gun, hanging on the peg.

"Don't do anything stupid, Sheriff," she advised. "I don't want to kill you, but I will."

"Then what—"

"Do you have any rope here?"

"Rope?" He frowned, then seemed to get it. "In that corner."

"Okay, into the cell block."

He obeyed, leading her into the block, which had three cells. She plucked the keys off another wall peg.

"Pick one," she said.

"What?"

"Well, it's your jail," she said. "You must know which one would be most comfortable."

He looked at all three cells for a moment, then said, "The middle one."

"Go ahead, then," she said. "Into the middle one."

He stepped in. She closed the door behind him, used the key to lock it.

"That's it?" he asked. "What now?"

"Just relax," she said. "We're not done."

***

By the time she was done he was tied, and gagged, lying on the pallet in the cell. Roxy left the cell block and locked that door with the key. Then walked out of the office and pulled the door closed. There hadn't been a key in the desk for it, so it would have to stay unlocked.

She was hoping that anyone looking for the sheriff would simply decide he wasn't there. If they tried to get into the cell block, the locked door would stop them. And they wouldn't be able to unlock it, because she was going to take the key with her and discard it somewhere.

Taggert couldn't yell, and couldn't move very well, as she had not only tied him up, she had tied him to the pallet, itself. He couldn't even roll off of it. She hoped that her efforts would give her enough time to find Wheeler, and face him without having Taggert as his back-up.

She looked up and down the street to see if anyone was watching her. People walked past, tossed her a glance, but no one seemed especially interested.

She stepped into the street, crossed over, and walked briskly away.

Chapter Forty-Two

With the sheriff taken care of, hopefully for at least the day, she started her search for Wheeler. Since he had found her the day before, she was hoping he'd be out in the open now, easy to find. By late afternoon she realized that was not to be the case. Either they simply had not crossed paths, or he had gone to ground, again, hiding from her until he was ready to make his move.

She decided going to the Live Oak Saloon might shake things up a bit, since that's where her impersonator apparently did her drinking.

As she entered she found it about half full, the hour still being rather early for many of the regulars who had jobs. The men there were the ones who didn't work, or were passing through.

She went to the bar and ordered a beer.

"Back again, huh?" Ted, the bartender said, as he set the beer in front of her.

"Does that surprise you?" she asked.

"Well, when you proved that the Lady Gunsmith grave was empty, some of us figured you'd leave town."

"Figured, or hoped?" she asked.

"I'll bet some hoped," he said, "and others figured. Me, I never like potential customers to leave town."

"I'm a customer, all right," she said. "But I'm glad you took down your sign."

"It'll stay down, too . . . unless you get shot, again."

She laughed and said, "I'll have another beer on that."

He brought her the second beer, leaned on the bar and said, "There's probably somethin' I should tell you."

"What's that?"

"There's two fellas sittin' at a back table, splittin' a bottle of whiskey."

She turned and looked at the two he meant, then looked back at him.

"So?"

"They're the two who are supposed to have gunned down Lady Gunsmith."

"Is that a fact?"

"I just thought you should know," he said, "but I'm hopin' you don't gun them down here."

"Why not?" she asked. "That'd get your Live Oak some publicity, wouldn't it?"

"Sure," he said, "as a place to go and get shot."

She looked at the two men again. They seemed unconcerned about anything.

"What's your play gonna be?" the bartender asked.

"I need to find the man they work for," she said, "so I think I'll just keep an eye on them."

Nick Owens and Carlos Montalvo were wishing they had never left the Wild Jack saloon.

"What do we do?" Montalvo asked when Roxy Doyle entered the saloon.

"Well, first of all," Owens said, "we don't know that it's her."

"Come on, Nick," Montalvo said. "How many women do you think look like that?"

"Well," Owens said, "so far, two. I actually thought it was Franny when she walked in."

"Well, it ain't," Montalvo said. Although he was Mexican by birth, Montalvo had no discernible accent. "That's the goddamned Lady Gunsmith."

"Yeah, you're probably right."

"So what do we do?" Montalvo asked. "Get out of here?'

"No," Owens said, "if we do that, we'll be obvious. She ain't comin' over here, so let's just take it easy and not panic."

"What if we kill 'er?" Montalvo asked. "Wouldn't that make Wheeler happy?"

"No, it wouldn't," Owens said. "He wants to do that himself."

"But he's payin' us to help him."

"Right," Owens said, "help. He's payin' us to back him when he makes his play."

"Well," Montalvo said, sourly, "he better make it soon."

"Don't look at her!" Owens growled.

Montalvo jerked his head back around and stared at his partner.

"Don't tell me what to do!"

"I'm just tellin' you not to ruin this for us," Owens said. "We get the rest of our money after she's dead."

"So let's kill 'er!" Montalvo said.

"We kill her now we don't get the rest of our money from Wheeler."

"So what?" Montalvo asked. "We'd be the men who killed goddamned Lady Gunsmith. We'd be makin' plenty of money, then."

Owens rubbed his jaw, thought about his partner's words.

"Come on," Montalvo said, "we can take 'er. She's just a phony legend pumped up by the newspapers. She's no goddamned Gunsmith!"

"Lemme think," Owens said, "just lemme think."

Chapter Forty-Three

Fran Dunston was doing some thinking of her own.

There had to be a way she could help her man, Jeff Wheeler, and make him realize that he was, truly, her man. And the only way she could think to do that was to kill Roxy Doyle.

She strapped on her gun, stood in front of the mirror, and drew several times. She was fast. That was one of the reasons Wheeler had chosen her for this job. She actually could outdraw some men in a fair gunfight, like that poor slob Homer Mason. He had to die just to make a point.

Well, maybe Roxy Doyle had to die to make a point.

She holstered the gun one last time, grabbed her hat, and left the house to walk back to town.

***

Jeff Wheeler entered the Wild Jack Saloon and didn't see Owens and Montalvo there. That worried him. Had those two idiots gone out to do something stupid.

He went to the bar and asked, "Where are the two fellas who usually sit at that table."

The bored looking bartender said, "They went out."

"I can see that," Wheeler said. "Do you have any idea where they went?"

"They said somethin' about drinkin' somewhere else."

"Why would they want to drink somewhere else?" Wheeler said, not really asking the bartender the question.

"Why wouldn't they?" the bartender answered, anyway. "You've seen this place."

"Crap," Wheeler said, still not talking to the bartender.

"Exactly," the barman said.

Wheeler turned and walked out without saying anything further. If those two idiots decided to go to the Live Oak, they could end up ruining everything he'd planned.

"I'm gettin' tired of waitin'," Montalvo said.

"I gotta think," Owens said.

"You keep sayin' that, Nick," Montalvo said, "but thinkin' ain't a strong point for either one of us. Doin' is!"

"You're right, I guess."

"Then let's do this."

Owens took one more second, then said, "Yeah, okay, let's do it."

They started to get up when the batwing doors opened and a red-haired woman entered.

"Oh boy," Owens said, sitting back down.

Roxy saw the two men start to get up, but then they stopped when the woman came through the batwing doors. She was surprised, but at the same time, pleased. Besides Wheeler, this was the other person she wanted to find.

She turned her back to the bar and waited.

Franny moved quickly through town, figuring if she was going to find Lady Gunsmith anywhere, it would be a saloon. She checked two before she got to the Live Oak and peered over the batwing doors. She saw the woman at the bar, and immediately stepped inside.

"I have to thank you," Roxy said.

"For what?" Fran asked.

"Not making me come looking for you."

"Jesus," the bartender said, from behind Roxy. "She does look a little like you. Maybe even a lot."

"At a distance, maybe," Roxy said. "You better move."

"Right, right," he said, "but watch those two in the back."

"Yeah, thanks."

The bartender moved out from behind the bar. Several men who were standing nearby also put some distance between themselves and Roxy.

"Is this a coincidence," Roxy asked, "or were you looking for me?"

"I was looking."

"What's your name?"

The woman looked flustered for a moment, then said, "Fran. What does that—"

"I just like to know people's names when I'm dealing with them," Roxy said. "So Fran, now that you found me, what do you intend to do?"

"I intend to kill you."

"So first you impersonate me, and now you want to kill me?" Roxy asked. "Why?"

"If I don't kill you," she said, "you'll kill the man I love."

"Wheeler?" Roxy asked.

"That's right."

"Really?" Roxy said. "You love him?"

"I do."

"Does he love you?"

Fran hesitated, then said, "I—I think so."

"So you're ready to kill for him, even though you only think he loves you."

"He does," Fran said. "He loves me."

"And are you ready to die for him?"

"Yes."

"Then you're a foolish woman."

"Let's just get this over with," Fran said.

"You're letting the fact that you impersonated me go to your head, Fran," Roxy said. "You can't beat me."

"We'll see, won't we?"

"We don't have to see," Roxy insisted. "Let Wheeler do his own dirty work."

"You're talkin' too much," Fran said.

"I'm trying to save your—" Roxy started, but Fran Dunston had heard enough. She went for her gun.

Roxy had to take a quick look at the two men in the back of the room. They were seated, and appeared to be staying that way.

As for Fran, she wasn't nearly fast enough to be doing what she was doing. But Roxy had no choice, so she drew and fired once. As the phony Lady Gunsmith crumpled to the floor, Roxy once again looked at the two men. They hadn't moved.

She turned and looked at the bartender.

"Should I send somebody for the sheriff?" he asked.

Normally, she would have said yes. "No, but have some-body take her to the undertaker's."

"Really?" the bartender asked. "No law?"

"No," she said, "not until this is over."

Chapter Forty-Four

As Fran Dunston's body was dragged out of the saloon, Roxy holstered her gun, and faced the two men in the back.

"What about you two?" she asked. "Are you next?"

"What?" Owens said.

"Us?" Montalvo asked. "Why would we—"

"Shut up! I know you work for Wheeler. If you're not going to stand up to me now, then get out, find Wheeler and tell him what happened. Tell him I'll be waiting for him here."

The two men jumped to their feet and headed for the doors.

"And if I was you," she called after them, "I wouldn't come back here with him."

"Yeah," Owens said, "right."

He and Montalvo went out the door.

Roxy looked at the bartender.

"Beer?" he asked.

"Oh, yeah," she said.

***

Wheeler had decided to simply wait at the Wild Jack Saloon for Owens and Montalvo to return, rather than wander around town looking for them. He didn't want to run into Roxy Doyle until he was good and ready. So rather than check at the Live Oak, he went back into the Wild Jack and sat with a beer, nursing it.

When the two men returned they did so on the run breathlessly. They went to the bar and ordered beers before they noticed Wheeler was there, waiting.

"Wheeler," Owens said.

Montalvo turned at the sound of the name and looked.

"Crap," he said.

"Where have you two been?"

"Wheeler," Owens said, walking to the table with his beer. Montalvo followed. "We're really sorry—"

"About what?" Wheeler demanded. "What did you do?"

"We didn't do anythin'," he insisted. "We just went to the Live Oak for a drink."

"We got bored sittin' here," Montalvo added.

"And then she just walked in, and—"

"Who walked in?"

"The girl, that lady Gunsmith," Owens said.

"Did you kill 'er?"

"No, we didn't, but—"

"Did you try to kill 'er. No, that would mean you were dead, and maybe you'll wish you were—"

"But then the other girl walked in," Montalvo said, cutting him off.

"What other girl?"

"You know, your girl," Owens said.

"The phony Lady Gunsmith," Montalvo said.

"Franny?" Wheeler asked. "Franny was at the Live Oak?"

"That's what we're tellin' ya," Owens said, taking a swallow of beer.

"What happened?" Wheeler asked.

"Well," Owens said, "she shot 'er."

"Shot 'er dead," Montalvo added.

"Wait a minute," Wheeler said. "Slow down. Who shot who?"

"The real Lady Gunsmith shot the fake Lady Gunsmith," Owens said. "Your girl."

"Shot 'er dead," Montalvo said again.

"Franny's dead?"

"That's what we're tellin' ya!" Owens said.

"And what did you two do?" Wheeler asked.

"We didn't do nothin'," Owens said. "You didn't want us to do nothin' until you was ready."

"Ain't that right?" Montalvo asked.

"That didn't mean," Wheeler said, "that I wanted you to stand by and watch Franny get shot."

"Well," Owens said, "we didn't think—"

"Where's Franny now?" Wheeler demanded, cutting the man off.

"They took her to the undertaker," Owens said.

"And what about the sheriff?"

"Nobody sent for him," Montalvo said.

"The Lady said she didn't want no law until this was all finished."

"Is that right?" Wheeler stood up.

"What are you gonna do?" Owens asked.

"Come with me," Wheeler said.

177

"Um," Montalvo said, "she, uh, told us not to go back there."

"She told you?"

"Well . . . yeah," Montalvo said.

"Who do you work for?"

"Um," Owens said, "we work for you, but—"

"Then get your goddamned asses up and come with me!" Wheeler shouted.

The two men jumped to their feet, Montalvo taking the time to grab his beer and finish it before following Wheeler and Owens out of the saloon.

Chapter Forty-Five

"So you're just gonna wait?" the big bartender asked.

"Your name's Bellamy, right?" she asked.

"That's right," Bellamy said.

"Well, Bellamy," she said, "I think the best thing for me to do now is stay put and wait, don't you?"

"I think you sent out enough of a callin' card," Bellamy said.

"We agree," she said.

"Any particular reason why you didn't want me to send somebody for the sheriff?"

"I happen to know that Sheriff Taggert is a bit tied up, at the moment. I don't think he'd be of any help."

"Uh-huh," Bellamy said. He looked around as the Live oak began to fill up. "Gets busy about this time, but it looks like it's gettin' even busier."

"I guess the word has gone out," she said. "They want to see if Lady Gunsmith is going to get killed—again."

"This time for real," Bellamy added. "I get the feelin' there's gonna be a lot of disappointed people in here when this is all over."

"That's what I'm hoping," she said.

"You don't have any back-up," Bellamy said. "What if they do come back with Wheeler?"

"That'll be too bad for them."

"Are you really as confident as you sound?" he asked.

"I'd have to be, wouldn't I?"

"Well," he said, reaching beneath the bar, "I've got this." He came out with a double-barrel, over-and-under Greener shotgun.

"No way," she said.

"Why not?"

"For one thing I hate over-and-under shotguns. The side-by-side barrels are more reliable. And for the second thing, I don't want you getting killed on account of me."

"Ain't that my lookout?" he asked.

"Look, I appreciate the offer," she said, "but I've got to say no."

"So you're gonna get my place all shot up and not give me a chance to play?"

She smiled at him. "I'll take it outside if I can. How's that?"

"I hope you don't think I'm lookin' for anythin' in return," he said. "I mean, you're beautiful and all, but I wouldn't want you to think—"

"I'm thinking you might just want to put up a new sign," she said.

Now he smiled. "You've got me pegged."

"I tell you what," she said. "Once I leave town, you can put up whatever kind of sign you like. Deal?"

"Deal."

They shook on it, and he put his shotgun back beneath the bar.

* * *

Jeff Wheeler opened the door to the sheriff's office and stormed in, followed by Owens and Montalvo.

"Sheriff!" he shouted. "Taggert!"

"He's not here," Owens observed.

Wheeler walked to the door of the cell block and tried it. He looked at the pegs on the wall. On one hung the sheriff's gunbelt. The other was empty. No keys.

"Locked," he said. "Find the keys."

They searched the desk, looked around the office, with no luck.

Wheeler banged on the door, but to no avail.

"You think he's locked in there?" Owens asked.

"Montalvo," Wheeler ordered, "go around and look in the cell windows."

"Right."

Wheeler and Owens waited for Montalvo to return. When he did he said, "He's in the middle cell, all trussed up. He can't get to the door. I think the cell is locked, too."

"She did it," Wheeler said. "Roxy Doyle. She took him out of the play."

"That leaves three of us," Owens said.

"Only because she killed Franny."

"So what do we do?" Montalvo asked.

"We're gonna kill 'er," Wheeler said, "just like I planned."

"She's fast, Wheeler," Owens said. "She killed your girl with no trouble. She never even cleared leather, and she was pretty fast."

"It doesn't matter how fast she is," Wheeler said. "Not the way I've got it planned."

"You got more men?" Owens asked, hopefully.

"No," Wheeler said, looking at the gun rack on the wall. "Break the lock on that rock and I'll tell you what I've got in mind.

Chapter Forty-Six

"Another beer?" Bellamy asked Roxy.

"No, thanks," she said. "I've got to keep my head on straight."

"You really think they'll be back?"

"They will, or Wheeler will. Maybe all three. This business of the three graves, it's going to end today."

"Three empty graves," Bellamy said, shaking his head. "Who woulda thunk it."

"Jeff Wheeler did," she said. "What I can't figure out is why I didn't hear of it before I rode in here."

"Coincidence?"

She made a face. "I hate that word, but I guess that was it."

"It don't matter," he said. "You woulda heard about it, anyway, sooner or later."

"And Wheeler would've been waiting," she said. 'Got himself a job as a bartender in Telegraph so he could blend in."

Bellamy looked around at the interior of the Live Oak. The place was jumping, and he had two girls working the floor.

"I'm doin' a helluva business right now," he said.

"Thanks to me, I'll bet."

"No bet," he said. "You're right. Say, mind if I ask you a question?"

"Go ahead."

"You didn't happen to kill the sheriff, didja?"

"Nope," she said. "When I said he was tied up, I meant it. That satisfy you?"

"Yeah, it does," Bellamy said. "I got you pegged as bein' in the right."

"I appreciate that," she said. "I'm just trying to make sure my name stays clear, and I don't like the thought of people thinking I'm dead, either."

"Alive and in the clear," Bellamy said, "that's the way to be. How about some coffee?'

"That'll do," she said.

He brought her a cup, tended to a couple of other customers, then came back and leaned on the bar.

"I got another question," he said, "since we're whilin' away the time."

"Go ahead."

"You really Gavin Doyle's daughter?"

"I am. Do you know him?"

"Heard of him," Bellamy said, "You hear lots of stories when you tend bar."

"I haven't heard where he might be, these days, have you?"

He rubbed his jaw. "I heard he was dead, but you don't wanna hear that, do ya?"

"Not hardly. I've been looking for him close to ten years, now. I haven't found hide nor hair of him, but I also haven't seen any proof that he's dead."

"You talk pretty educated," he said.

"It's a sham," she said. "I grew up poor, went out on my own at fifteen and have been educating myself ever since. I just don't want to sound ignorant."

"Well, you don't," Bellamy said. "And I'd know, because in this job I run into plenty of ignorant people. Plus I'm pretty ignorant, myself."

"I doubt that," she said. "Like me, I bet you've got your own kind of education."

He laughed. "You're probably right. I just never thought of it that way."

Roxy looked around. Plenty of the people in the saloon were looking her way, probably wondering when the action was going to commence, and what the outcome would be?

"I hope this goes the way we want," she said to Bellamy, "for both of us."

"I'll keep my fingers crossed," Bellamy said.

Chapter Forty-Seven

Roxy was drinking a second cup of coffee when Jeff Wheeler entered the Live Oak. Immediately, the saloon went quiet. Roxy put down her cup and turned to face the door. Wheeler stood just inside. It was so silent that she heard every sound the batwing doors made until they finally stopped swinging behind him.

"Alone?" she asked.

"Why not?" he answered, spreading his hands.

"I just figured," she said, "that if you were anything like your brother, you'd travel in a pack."

"Like a wolf?" he asked.

"Like a coward."

His face turned red, but he held his temper.

"There are a lot of people in here," he said. "Somebody could get hurt."

"The street is fine with me," she said.

"I'll be outside," Wheeler said. He turned and went back out the doors.

Roxy looked at Bellamy.

"You know what that means, don't you?"

"I do," she said. "Pour me another cup of coffee, will you? I'll be back before it gets cold."

"Of course," he said.

She walked to the batwing doors and looked out over them. Wheeler was standing in the middle of the street, which was otherwise empty. People had already begun to gather across the way, and behind her she could hear men taking bets.

She stepped through the doors.

"Right there?" Wheeler asked. "Really? There'll be some damage to the building, and maybe to someone inside."

She smiled. "You're assuming you'll get off a shot."

"Oh," he said, "I'll get off a shot."

Roxy's every instinct was heightened. As she stepped into the street she could even feel the slight breeze on her skin. She was acutely aware of everything around her.

She moved to the center of the street, stopped about ten paces away from Wheeler.

"You went through a lot of trouble to get me here," she said.

"And it wasn't even necessary," he said, "since you rode in, anyway."

"I can't believe that," she said. "You must have known I was in New Mexico, to even start your plan in motion."

Wheeler smiled. "You're a smart girl. I had all four borders covered. I knew exactly when you crossed from Arizona into New Mexico."

"I thought so," she said, although it was more like she'd hoped so. The coincidence of it was just too much to accept. Now she knew.

"I knew how long it would take you to get here," he went on. "I knew what three towns to use."

"You couldn't have known that," she said. "I didn't even know where I was going."

"I paid a lot of money to have your movements predicted," he said, "according to where you entered New Mexico, what direction you would most likely ride in, what kind of horse you were on . . ."

"I hope it was worth all the money you spent," she said.

"It doesn't matter," he said. "I have more, lots more."

"Then you should be off somewhere spending it, enjoying it," she said. "Not here, dying on the street in some nothing town."

"You and me," he said, "we're gonna turn this town into something. The place where the real Lady Gunsmith died."

"Do it, then," she said. "Let's get it done with."

She was close enough to him to watch not only his shoulders, but his eyes as well. They flicked, twice, left and right.

And then he drew.

Her first shot struck him in the chest, just below his chin. She didn't wait to see if he went down. She knew he would.

She dropped to one knee, turned right, shot Owens right off the roof of the saloon.

Then she turned left, swiveling on that knee, and shot Montalvo, knocking him back from the window he'd been leaning out of.

The street was quiet. All the people to her right, across the street, and all those people pressed up against the windows and doorway of the saloon, had been holding their breath. Now they released it, but made no other sound. They were all stunned by her speed, and ability.

She walked to the fallen Wheeler, ejecting the empty cartridges from her gun and reloading as she went. When she reached him, she holstered the gun and looked down. There was no need to lean over and check. He was dead.

She heard the batwings swing open and saw Bellamy step out, shotgun in hand. She walked over to him, held out the keys to the sheriff's cell block, which she had decided to keep on her rather than toss away.

"Can you have somebody go and let the sheriff out of his jail?" she asked.

"Sure." He accepted the keys.

"Then tell him where the other two men are," she said. "He can have somebody clean up."

"Where are you going?" he asked.

"Away," she said. "Away from here."

Chapter Forty-Eight

Roxy drew circles with her finger across the black skin of Conrad's flat belly. They were in bed in a hotel room in Telegraph.

"You're leaving today?" he asked.

"Yup." She reached down and took hold of his huge penis. "I only came back yesterday for one more time with this."

As she stroked it, it started to grow hard again.

"Well," he said, his breath coming more quickly, "I might have something else for you."

She sat up, took his penis in both hands and continued to caress it.

"What more could you have for me than this?" she asked.

"I might have some . . . news."

She was pumping him faster and faster, and still he swelled, not yet at full size and hardness.

"What kind of news?"

She could feel him getting close, so she didn't stop.

"There was a man . . . here yesterday . . ." he almost panted. "He . . . said something about . . . having seen . . . Ohhhhh . . ."

Suddenly, his penis erupted and a geyser of white shot into the air. Roxy had to scramble back so she wouldn't get soaked by it. It landed on the sheets, and on him, the color of pearls against his black skin.

"Jesus, woman!" he said, running his big hand over his face.

"That didn't take long," she said.

"Because you have those kind of hands," he told her. "You play a man like a good piano player plays the piano."

"That's a nice compliment," she said. "Now, what about this news?"

"A man was here yesterday, and he said—stop that, woman!" He slapped her hand away from his penis. "He said he'd heard something about Gavin Doyle being in Oregon."

"Oregon?" she asked, suddenly ignoring his body. "That far north?"

"That's what he said."

"What else did he say?"

"Nothing," Conrad replied.

"Why did he even bring it up?"

"He said he'd heard that Lady Gunsmith had been killed here," Conrad said. "Mandy straightened him out on that. Then he said he knew you were Gavin Doyle's daughter, and that even though he'd heard Doyle was dead, he'd heard something about him being in Oregon, recently."

"What part of Oregon?" she demanded.

"He didn't say."

"Well, who was this man?" she asked. "Where can I find him?"

"He's gone," Conrad said. "He rode out yesterday, going West."

Roxy jumped out of bed and started to get dressed.

191

"He only has one day's head start on me, then. What was his name?"

"We don't always get names at the whorehouse," he said, watching her dress.

"Well, what did he look like?"

"He was tall, thin, in his forties—"

"That's a lot of men!" she complained.

"You'll recognize him," Conrad said. "He's missing both front teeth."

"That's good!" she exclaimed, strapping on her gun. "I've got to go, Conrad."

"I know," he said. "Have some breakfast."

"I'll have it on the trail."

She headed for the door, then turned to look at him.

"Wait a minute," she said. "Were you going to let me leave New Mexico without this information?"

"Of course not!"

"Then how were you going to get it to me?"

He grinned at her, showing very white teeth, and took his flaccid penis in hand.

"I knew you'd be back . . . for this!"

She stared at his cock, which was getting hard again in his own hand.

"You're a very bad man, Conrad," she said, and hurried out the door before she changed her mind.

Coming August 2017

Lady Gunsmith 3
Roxy Doyle and The Shanghai Saloon

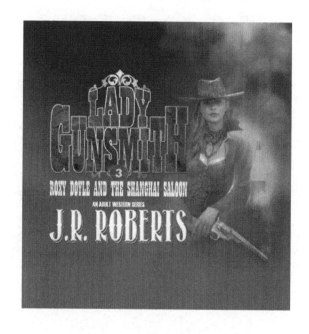

By
AWARD-WINNING AUTHOR
J.R. Roberts

For more information
visit: www.speakingvolumes.us

ANGEL EYES *series*
by
Award-Winning Author
Robert J. Randisi (J.R. Roberts)

Visit us at www.speakingvolumes.us

TRACKER *series*
by
Award-Winning Author
Robert J. Randisi (J.R. Roberts)

Visit us at www.speakingvolumes.us

MOUNTAIN JACK PIKE *series*
by
Award-Winning Author
Robert J. Randisi (J.R. Roberts)

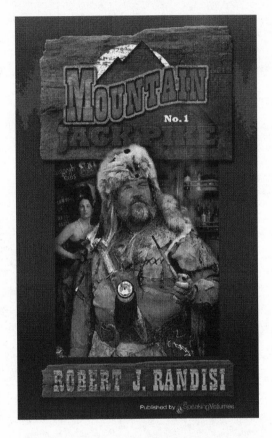

Visit us at www.speakingvolumes.us

Sign up for free and bargain books

Join the Speaking Volumes mailing list

Text

ILOVEBOOKS

to 22828 to get started.

Message and data rates may apply.